from the library of

DAVID AARON

Published in the United States of America
by Rand McNally & Company, 1985

© Grisewood & Dempsey Limited, 1981

Printed in Spain
by Graficas Reunidas SA, Madrid.

ISBN 0-528-82166-0
Library of Congress Catalog Card Number: 85-61170

RAND McNALLY

History
Encyclopedia

RAND McNALLY & COMPANY
Chicago · New York · San Francisco

Contents

EDITORIAL
Deborah Manley
Andrew Sich
Cover: Denise Gardner

Life before Man

Many strange creatures lived on Earth before people. The dinosaurs ruled the planet for 100 million years – fifty times longer than we have been here.

Early amphibian

Some of the first animals that lived in the sea.

STONE BONES

We know about the animals that lived before people from fossils. Fossils are the remains of animals that have been preserved in the rocks. When they died, the soft parts of the animals decayed. The bones sank into the mud. There they slowly turned to stone. Millions of years later people found the stone bones, chipped them from the rocks, and put them all back together. From animals that are alive today, we can guess what they must have looked like.

Life in the Sea

About 600 million years ago life appeared in the sea. Tiny plants and soft creatures, like blobs of jelly, floated in the waves. Soon there were many animals. Huge sea scorpions grabbed other animals in their great claws. Giant creatures like octopuses strangled their victims with tentacles that came out from their hard shells. Fishes had thick armor to defend them from these monsters.

From Fins to Feet

The first life on land were plants that grew by the water's edge. Fish swam into the shallows to feed. Some of them started to breathe out of water. They had strong fins with which they pushed themselves onto land. On land there were no enemies to eat them. They stayed there and became the first land animals—amphibians. But they could not go far from the water. They still needed water to lay their eggs in.

Brontosaurus, a giant plant eater.

Plesiosaur

Ichthyosaur

Pteranodon was a
flying reptile.

Tyrannosaurus, the
fiercest of all dinosaurs.

Two plant-eating dinosaurs. Stego-
saurus defended itself with its club-like
tail. Triceratops charged its enemies
with its horns.

The Dreaded Dinosaurs
The first animals that could lay eggs
on land were the reptiles. The greatest
of these were the dinosaurs. The word
dinosaur means 'terrible lizard', but
although many dinosaurs were huge,
few were terrible. Most of them were
peaceful plant-eaters. Brontosaurus
weighed 30 tons. It was more than 65
feet long, but it could only move slowly,
spending its time eating to fill its great
stomach.

The fiercest dinosaur was the meat-
eating Tyrannosaurus. It was 20 feet
high and ran on its back legs. It held
its prey while it sank its dagger-like
teeth into them.

The Death of the Dinosaurs
The dinosaurs ruled the world and
then suddenly died out. We do not
know why. Perhaps the world
became too cold for them. The animals
that took their place were mammals, and the most successful of all
the mammals was man.

Archaeopteryx was the first known
bird. It evolved from reptiles and was
like them in many ways. It had teeth
in its beak, scales on its head and
claws on its wings.

The hairy mammoth was a mammal.
It lived in the Ice Age after the
dinosaurs were extinct.

Finding out about History

We learn about people of long ago by studying what they left behind them. Sometimes these remains are easy to see, like the pyramids of Egypt or even the machinery of the last century. But a vast amount of material is buried under the ground.

Archaeology: the study of the past
Experts unearth the remains that are buried. They can then get a better idea of how people centuries ago really lived. This type of study has a special name: *archaeology*. The men and women who dig up the past are called *archaeologists*.

Sometimes archaeologists discover rich hoards of gold and silver. But even a small piece of pottery can give important clues to the life its owner led and how he or she worked.

An Archaeological Dig
The work on an archaeological 'dig' is a combination of heavy manual work (removing the covering layers) and great care (sifting and sorting the finds). It is very important that each discovery is recorded and preserved as it emerges from under the ground.

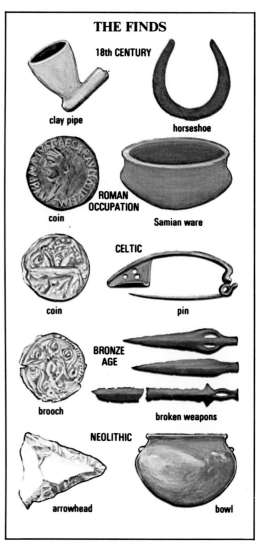

THE FINDS

18th CENTURY

clay pipe

horseshoe

coin

ROMAN OCCUPATION

Samian ware

CELTIC

coin

pin

brooch

BRONZE AGE

broken weapons

NEOLITHIC

arrowhead

bowl

Dating the Finds

Any place where people have lived for a long time has a record of the life of those people. Later settlements were often built on the ruins of earlier settlements (just as new buildings are built on cleared sites today). In this way the site is built up in a series of layers.

In an undisturbed site, the layers at the bottom must be older than those above. From knowing which layer an object came from, an archaeologist can date it, and can get a complete history of the site from the first to the last people who lived there.

Left: The ancient Egyptians in their wall paintings and other records, gave us a very detailed picture of life in their day. Here, we see a religious ceremony called the 'Opening of the Mouth', a ceremony performed to allow the dead person to breathe and eat in the life after death in which the Egyptians believed.

Below and left: These pictures give an idea of what an archaeologist might hope to find. A trench is cut into an ancient site somewhere in Europe. People have lived here from the Stone Age onwards. Their remains have been laid down in layers. At the very bottom are objects used by Stone Age hunters. The Bronze Age level contains broken weapons. Post holes from Celtic times are the remains of a wooden stockade or fence. The Roman conquerors built a strong defensive wall on the site. In a real site the layers would be jumbled up where later people had dug wells, graves, ditches and rubbish pits.

Discovering more Recent History

When we want to find out about the more recent past (say, the last 1,000 years), we have a greater number of sources. These include written material (letters, diaries, government papers, records of meetings, old newspapers, novels and auto-biographies). There is also material like portraits, houses and factories, and, more recently, photographs and films.

These all add up to tell the historian about what was happening at a particular time and what people living at that time thought about the life around them.

We can also learn about history from people alive today. We can learn from their own memories and from the stories passed down to them by their parents and grandparents.

The Historian of the Future

In the future the historian is going to have an even greater mass of material to work through. This is because we now record so much of what is going on in our world. There will be television programs, home movies, magazine articles and computer records which will have to be dug into to find the facts of history.

The First People

The first human beings like us lived on Earth about 50,000 years ago. Humans have become the most important animals on Earth.

In 1859 an English scientist, Charles Darwin, suggested that the literal interpretation of the biblical story of Adam and Eve was wrong. Human beings had not appeared suddenly on Earth. They had developed over millions of years and were distantly related to apes and monkeys. Since then scientists have found many fossil bones and other remains of human-like creatures. These have supported Darwin's theory of evolution.

Down from the Trees
Some scientists think that about 70 million years ago our ancestors might have been small, furry animals much like tree shrews. Very slowly they became more like humans. Their faces became less pointed and their brains larger. They still lived in trees, using their hands to pluck fruit and leaves.

Millions of years ago our ancestors may have been like tree shrews.

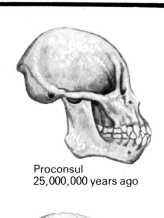

Proconsul
25,000,000 years ago

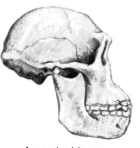

Australopithecus
5,000,000 years ago

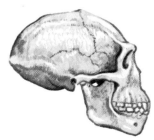

Homo erectus
1,000,000 years ago

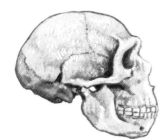

Neanderthal
100,000 years ago

Cro-Magnon
50,000 years ago

Changes in the shape of the human skull are shown in fossil remains. They help trace the history of Man.

Homo erectus was an early kind of man. He used simple tools to search for roots and grubs in the soil. He used fire to cook his food.

About 25 million years ago the Earth began to change. Great areas of forest disappeared. It became difficult for tree-dwelling animals to find homes and food. By this time our ancestors looked rather like large chimpanzees. Some of their descendants stayed in the trees. They became the apes. Others learned to live on the ground. They became human beings.

These early human-like creatures began to walk upright, and could now use their hands for carrying things. Their brains gradually became larger and so they became cleverer than other animals. They learned how to make tools and weapons, and how to use fire.

Thinking Man
About 100,000 years ago people called Neanderthal men were living in Europe. They were short and stocky with big brow ridges and powerful teeth. Their brains were as large as ours. They wore clothes and could make tools and weapons. Scientists named them *Homo sapiens* or 'thinking men.' This is

Above: Neanderthals hunted animals for food. In groups they could kill large prey.

MAN THE TOOL-MAKER

Primitive ape-like men were using tools some 1,750,000 years ago. These tools were made from stones, with one side chipped away until it was sharp. They could be used for chopping meat or shaping wood. As men developed they made better and sharper stone tools. They learned how to make a wooden spear stronger by hardening the tip in a fire. They fixed stone blades on wooden and bone handles to make axes, spears, and harpoons.

Right: Cro-Magnon artists used charcoal and colored earth to paint pictures on cave walls.

the group we belong to. But Neanderthal men were not our ancestors. Another group developed about 50,000 years ago. They were the first truly modern men. We call those who came to Europe Cro-Magnon men. They took the place of the Neanderthals.

They knew how to make weapons and build shelters. They could speak, paint and carve. They had started to control their world.

Life in the Stone Age

During the Stone Age, up to about 10,000 years ago, many people lived in caves. We learn about how they lived from the things they left behind.

At this time the climate of the Earth was colder than it is now. So caves made warm homes. Fires could be lit at the cave entrance, out of the wind. A blazing fire kept the cave-dwellers warm. It also scared off wild animals. During the cold Ice Ages many people lived in the warmer lands of southern France and Spain. Caves in the rocks where they lived can still be seen there. There was plenty of food. The rivers were full of fish. There were herds of reindeer, wild horses, woolly mammoths, musk oxen and other animals on the grassy plains. Hunting was easy. Probably people followed the herds, living in one cave in winter and another in summer.

Inside the Cave
Some caves were divided into 'rooms' by stone walls. Others had inner tents of skin. Large stones were used as tables and chairs. There were even stone 'carpets' made of small pebbles. The people slept on beds of animal skins, dried grass, and bracken. Their clothes, too, were made from animal skins. They cooked their meat in ovens made of pebbles mixed with clay, sand and

Cave dwellers were skillful craftsmen. They made tools such as bone needles, scrapers, knives, arrowheads and borers for making holes. They often carved animal figures out of bones or antlers too.

bone needle

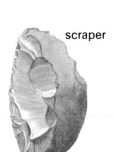

scraper

knife

arrowhead

borer

In Stone Age times no one could be lazy. Everyone, young and old, had to work hard, and help each other, to stay alive. The men went hunting, while the rest of the family scraped skins, gathered firewood, made tools from flint and bone, and tended the fire to keep them warm and to warn off wild animals. It was a busy life, and often a very hard one.

Farming began in the warm lands of the Middle East. Here people herded animals and planted wheat. Now they did not need to move about in search of food. They built houses and began to settle down.

limestone. In one such oven the remains of a Stone Age meal were found: bones from a mountain bear were resting in the oven on a bed of charcoal.

The men's main job was hunting. Some of the family prepared skins and furs, and sewed them together with bone needles to make clothes. Others made tools, sharpening pieces of flint by chipping and grinding.

They fixed flints to bones, horns or branches to make spears and harpoons. They used the fat scraped from animal skins as fuel in stone lamps. Animal skulls were used as pots and dishes. Large bones were used as anvils and chopping blocks. Small bones were turned into hand tools.

The people of the Stone Age were skillful artists. Deep inside their caves they painted pictures of the animals they hunted. Probably these paintings had a religious or magical meaning. They were made to bring the hunters good luck.

The End of the Ice age

By about 10,000 BC the ice covering northern Europe had melted. The plains became covered with forest. Many animals moved north to the colder regions. Many hunters followed, living in skin tents like American Indian tepees. In the Middle East, too, it was getting warmer. There were fewer animals to hunt. So people learned a new way of life. They gathered wild grain. Then they began to grow it for themselves. They tamed goats and wild sheep. These people became the first farmers.

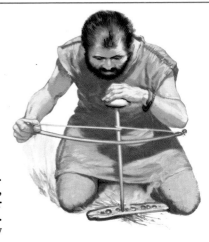

Fire was probably discovered accidentally. When certain stones are rubbed together, they send out sparks. If this is done near tinder-dry wood, a fire can be kindled. Right: Using a bow drill was a quicker way of making sparks.

The Most Important Inventions

We take many things, like lighting a fire or like wheels, for granted. But early people had to discover these things for themselves. Making fire was one of the most important inventions of all time.

With the discovery of fire people could cook meat and vegetables so that they became more tender and tasty. Most food was roasted on a spit. Fire was also important for the heat it gave out in the cold winter months, and for scaring off wild animals at night.

The earliest clothes were the skins and furs of the animals that had been killed. But as early as 8,000 years ago cloth is known to have been spun and woven in Western Asia. Thread was spun from flax or wool on a spindle twirled in the hand. It was then woven into cloth on primitive looms.

Early Use of Metals

Copper was the first metal to be discovered. People found that, when heated, it could be worked into different shapes. This gave a greater flexibility than was ever possible with stone. By mixing copper with tin, a harder metal (bronze) was made. This was in common use 4,000 years ago.

About a thousand years later, the Iron Age began. The smelting and forging of iron enabled craftsmen to make objects of great strength in any shape they cared to devise. Iron weapons for attack and armor for defense were very important in the battles that began to take place between

Left: Pottery was one of the earliest inventions. At first clay was molded simply by the potter's hands. Later the invention of the first wheel, the potter's wheel, allowed much better pots to be made more quickly.

Teamwork made difficult tasks simpler. Blocks of stone could be pulled more easily with rollers beneath them. From these rollers the first wheeled transport was probably devised.

peoples jealous of each other's riches. But iron was also important in agriculture. In particular the invention of the plow led to more efficient planting of seeds. This led to more abundant harvests.

In Sumer in the Middle East farmers discovered that, by digging ditches and making earth banks, they could control the flooding of rivers. Water was channeled off to drier lands and thus irrigation was discovered.

Writing and Paper

The people of Sumer were also the first writers. They wrote with wedge-shaped marks on clay tablets. They also worked out a way of doing calculations, by counting in 60s. They also used weights and measures. They were also the first people to devise a calendar. This was based on the phases of the moon, and gave them a year of twelve months. It was the Babylonians, however, who first used a seven-day week.

Paper was another of the great early inventions. Clay tablets were heavy and bulky, and had to be baked once they had been written on. The Chinese examined how wasps constructed their nests. They copied their method to make a form of paper. But even earlier than this the Egyptians had been using the reed papyrus which grew abundantly on the banks of the river Nile. They shaved the stalks into thin slices. They then pressed these into sheets not unlike paper. This invention was of great importance. Now records could be kept and messages could be sent accurately over long distances.

Above: The development of farming led to more settled communities. Cave life had suited the independent hunters but now it was necessary to have a permanent shelter near where the animals grazed and the crops grew. People saw that the sun baked mud hard. They learned to use baked mud to build houses. At first a frame was made from the entwined branches of trees. Mud was daubed on this frame to keep out the wind and the rain. About 6,000 years ago small round houses with curved roofs were built in Mesopotamia in this fashion. They looked like large beehives. In marshy country houses were often built on stilts. In later years mud was poured into molds and thus regular-shaped bricks were formed. With these mud bricks people could build much stronger, more long-lasting houses. Gradually, small towns grew up. Walls were built round them to protect the people inside from thieves and wild animals. Usually towns were centers for trade and markets were held at regular intervals so that people could come to buy and sell goods. They were also centers for religion and large temples were often built within their walls.

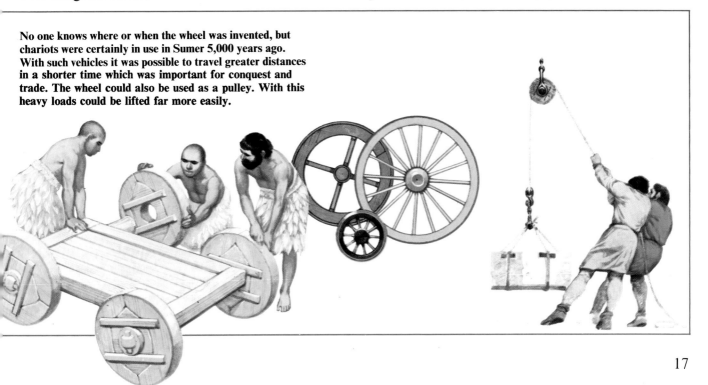

No one knows where or when the wheel was invented, but chariots were certainly in use in Sumer 5,000 years ago. With such vehicles it was possible to travel greater distances in a shorter time which was important for conquest and trade. The wheel could also be used as a pulley. With this heavy loads could be lifted far more easily.

People of Long Ago

In prehistoric times people learned about their past from legends. Now we learn about these people from the work of archaeologists.

Accurate history could not exist until people invented writing. The Sumerians, who lived around the great rivers of Mesopotamia, were probably the first to have a written language. But their records tell us very little about how they lived.

It is not until we come to the ancient Greeks that historians kept careful records of events.

Ancient Science and Art

Ancient peoples first used stone, then copper tools. Later they used bronze. Simple bronze tools were used to build the great pyramids of Egypt. Iron was not used until later.

The Egyptians had doctors who studied the human body to find out how it works. But the Greeks were the first people to use the science of medicine as we know it.

The Romans followed the Greeks as rulers of the Mediterranean world. They copied much from the Greeks. They are mostly remembered for being great builders, and good soldiers and rulers.

1: The Aztecs were warriors who made human sacrifices at religious events. They learned architecture and art from the Maya Indians and built cities.

2: The early people in Britain were farmers or hunters. They had only stone tools. They built huge rings of stones as temples to the sun.

3: The Maya Indians were skilled in farming, astronomy and mathematics. They could write and they built cities and huge stone pyramids.

4: The Romans were fine soldiers and good engineers. They built the greatest empire of the ancient world.

5: The Benin kingdom in West Africa once controlled the African slave trade. They made beautiful bronze figures.

6: At its greatest, the land of the Incas covered a huge part of South America. They were skillful potters, weavers and metalworkers.

7: In the forests of Central Africa there is a mysterious group of ruins called Zimbabwe. It is thought that the people who lived there traded with other nations.

8: The Phoenicians traded around the Mediterranean in their ships. They gave us the alphabet.

9: The great civilization of China developed from farming communities. They invented printing and how to make silk.

10: At Mohenjo-Daro in the valley of the Indus in northern India was a long-forgotten civilization.

11: The peaceful Minoans grew rich through trade. They built splendid palaces.

12: The warlike Assyrians had a fine army and horse-drawn chariots. Their capital, Ninevah, had the first library.

13: The Ancient Greeks are famed sculptors and writers. They had the first democracy and started the Olympic Games.

14: The story of the Hebrews is told in the Old Testament. They were farmers who came from Mesopotamia and settled in Palestine.

15: King Hammurabi made Babylon a center of learning. Scholars studied astronomy and mathematics. He wrote the first code of law.

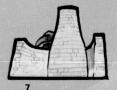

16: The Persians won a huge empire with their strong army. They built a road 1,616 miles long from the Mediterranean to the Arabian Gulf.

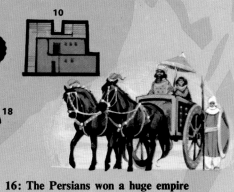

17: The Egyptian civilization lasted 27 centuries. They used a calendar like ours, designed the first clock and made paper. Their engineers built great burial pyramids.

18: As long ago as 3000 BC the Sumerians of the fertile land of Mesopotamia had a written language. They drove wheeled carriages, used metal made pots and wove cloth.

The Earliest Cities

Civilizations, where people lived in towns, grew up in places where the warm, fertile land could provide them with a good living.

Above: Great civilizations grew up in the fertile lands around the rivers shown on the map.

The Tigris and Euphrates

The Sumerian civilization was one of the first civilizations. It flourished 6,000 years ago in Mesopotamia, between the Tigris and Euphrates rivers. The rivers were rich in fish.

Left: This woman is grinding grain into flour with a stone. Crops not needed by the Sumerians themselves would be traded for other goods.

The empire of the warlike Assyrians lasted from the 900s to the 600s BC. Their kings rode to battle in chariots. In the background below is a ziggurat.

Their waters made the land fertile for crops. The pastures fed the herds of sheep, goats and cattle. These animals provided the people with meat, milk and wool. The Babylonians, Assyrians and others who later lived in the area also thrived because of the Tigris and Euphrates.

The City of Ur

Ur was one of the greatest of the cities of Sumer. It was surrounded by rich farmlands irrigated by a system of dikes and canals. Using plows drawn by oxen, the people of Ur could grow more food because they could cultivate more land.

Within the city, the Sumerians built huge palaces for their kings and a massive temple called a ziggurat. This was built by the Sumerian king Ur-Nammu. It had three terraces and long flights of steps led from ground level to the temple and gardens at the top.

Kings and rich people wore jewelry and beautifully embroidered robes. They lived in homes decorated with fine ornaments and statues. They kept servants and slaves. We know this from their tombs, as the rich were buried with their slaves and household goods.

Cuneiform Writing

The Sumerians learned to write *cuneiform* (wedge-shaped) letters on baked clay tablets with hard reeds. From these tablets we learn how Mesopotamian merchants did business, and about the laws and the deeds of the kings. Important government records were kept in a stone 'book' made from tablets hinged together in a wooden frame.

Scribes in Mesopotamia wrote on clay tablets. They used a kind of wedge-shaped writing called cuneiform. Many of these tablets have been dug up by archaeologists. They tell us a great deal about what life was like for the people of these early civilizations.

The End of Sumer

Other tribes were jealous of the wealth of Sumer and they attacked and burned their cities. At last the Sumerians were conquered by their enemies from a city to the north called Babylon.

Babylonians and Assyrians

The new kings had to fight to defend their territory and their water supplies. Their soldiers fought with spears, pikes, axes, javelins, and bows and arrows. Most of these weapons were made of bronze. They were no match for the iron swords and spears used by the Assyrians. In 689 BC King Sennacherib led a powerful army against Babylon. The attack and the siege of the city lasted for nine months.

China and Japan

Confucius

Shang pottery and bronze

Great Wall of China

Shang chariot and spearman

Top: The Great Wall of China was built 2,200 years ago to stop fierce Mongol tribesmen from attacking China. Confucius, born in 551 BC, was China's greatest philosopher. The Shang Dynasty ruled China 3,500 years ago; some of their pottery and bronze and a spearman with a chariot are shown here.

Above: Boats on the Hwang Ho, where Chinese civilization began.

The great civilizations of China and Japan were well advanced when Europe was still in the Stone Age.

In China, as elsewhere, civilization grew up around a great river. Here it was the Hwang Ho, or Yellow River. About 4000 BC people grew crops (millet and wheat, and later rice) along its banks. They kept cattle, and learned how to make silk from the cocoon of the silkworm.

About 3,500 years ago, the Chinese built great cities, with beautiful carvings in stone, jade and ivory. There, in workshops, craftsmen made ornaments of bronze and jeweled pendants in the shape of dragons, tigers, and other animals. Potters made fine pottery decorated with delicate designs and dragon faces.

Most people were peasant farmers and worked hard. They looked up to their emperor as a god who had to be obeyed. There were harsh punishments for disobedience and crime.

The Island People
Many thousands of years ago people from China moved into what is now Korea. Then they crossed to the islands of Japan. Other people came to Japan from the Pacific islands. The

Japanese borrowed ideas from the Chinese, including their calendar, their way of writing, one of their religions (Buddhism) and their system of government.

The Samurai
By the AD 1200s a group of powerful warriors known as the *samurai* ruled Japan.

These well-armed, mounted men were pledged to fight for truth and honor. People respected and feared them. If a samurai passed by, ordinary people had to fall to their knees and bow. If they did not, they might have their heads cut off.

Sport and Art
Both the Chinese and Japanese made fighting into a sport. This was how sports like *kung-fu*, *ju-jitsu*, and *kendo* developed. In kung-fu and ju-jitsu the fighters are unarmed; in kendo people fight with wooden swords.

The Japanese also loved the arts. They painted delicate pictures and decorated screens. As lovers of nature, they made gardens in which trees, flowers, sand, rocks and pools were arranged to look like living paintings.

Right: Samurai warriors wore frightening armor.

Chinese temple

Japanese temple

tori

farmhouse

Left: A Chinese temple, or pagoda. Above: A temple in Japan. In front are a tori, or gateway, and a simple farmhouse.

Shinto priests

Above: Shinto (teaching of the gods) was Japan's form of Buddhism.

samurai warriors

23

Everyday Life in Ancient China

For thousands of years the people of China lived differently from the rest of the world. Cut off by mountains, rivers, deserts and seas, they developed their own way of life.

In China, 3,000 years ago, there were many different chiefs or kings. They fought each other for lands and power. One of the most powerful families were the Shang kings. Wars were common and huge armies fought bloody battles in which thousands of men were killed. These ancient soldiers wore helmets and carried shields. They often rode into battle on horseback. Whole armies were sometimes killed when they were captured. Sometimes the soldiers completely destroyed a defeated town.

It was not until 221 BC that relative peace came to China when one king, Ch'in, defeated all the others and was declared Emperor. To keep foreign armies out of China, the Emperor ordered a wall to be built along the whole length of the northern border. When it was finished it stretched for over 1,800 miles.

Town Life

Towns in ancient China were centers for trade, learning and government. They were usually surrounded by high walls and were carefully planned. Craftsmen had their own quarter and produced pottery and metal goods in their workshops. Houses of the wealthy were built around courtyards and the larger ones had gardens. Most poor people, however, lived in shacks with mud walls and thatched roofs.

Gods and Thinkers

The Chinese were not forced to believe in one God. Many followed the teachings of Confucius, who said people should obey rules of behavior and respect those of higher rank. Others were Taoists, whose religion stressed simplicity and humility, or Buddhists, who believed people should give up everything they desired.

Market places grew up near the main gates of a town. Peasants from the country brought their produce to exchange for other goods. While there they might have their hair cut or pay taxes to their local lord.

What people wore

Poor people in China wore a simple tunic, tied at the waist, and a pair of trousers. In winter, which could be bitterly cold, they wore sheepskins or tunics made from padded cloth. Rich people wore garments made of silk. These were beautifully decorated with embroidery or gold leaf. It seems that the Chinese nearly always wore some sort of hat or headdress. On their feet the peasants wore rough sandals, while the rich had boots and shoes made from leather.

Art and fine craftsmanship

Artists carved animals, dragons and demons on wood and stone. They also made figures from a green stone called jade, and drew scenes from country life on silk and paper. Pottery was one of the first crafts in ancient China and the potters were skilled at producing vessels of great beauty which were obviously intended for daily use. Later, craftsmen also produced beautiful objects in bronze.

Below: Work on a typical small farm in China during the Spring. Water for the crops was all-important. Canals criss-crossed the fields. There were machines for scooping water out of them. Operated by pedals, a chain of scoops lifted the water from the canal. There is also a well from which water was raised in buckets. The buckets were then transported at either end of a pole on the back of one of the farmhands. Here, in the court-yard, the buildings are being re-plastered. This work was normally undertaken in the Spring. In the fields oxen pulled a plow while farmhands scattered seed in the furrows. On the left, young plants are being tended. The main crops in northern China were wheat, millet and hemp, while in the south rice was the chief food. Hemp was used to make cloth and rope and its seeds could be eaten when other crops failed. During the summer some of the farmers would hoe and tend the crops while others would make silk. The silk came from silk-worms or moth caterpillars. In the autumn the harvest was reaped and taken to a granary. This was usually built on stilts to keep out the damp and the rats.

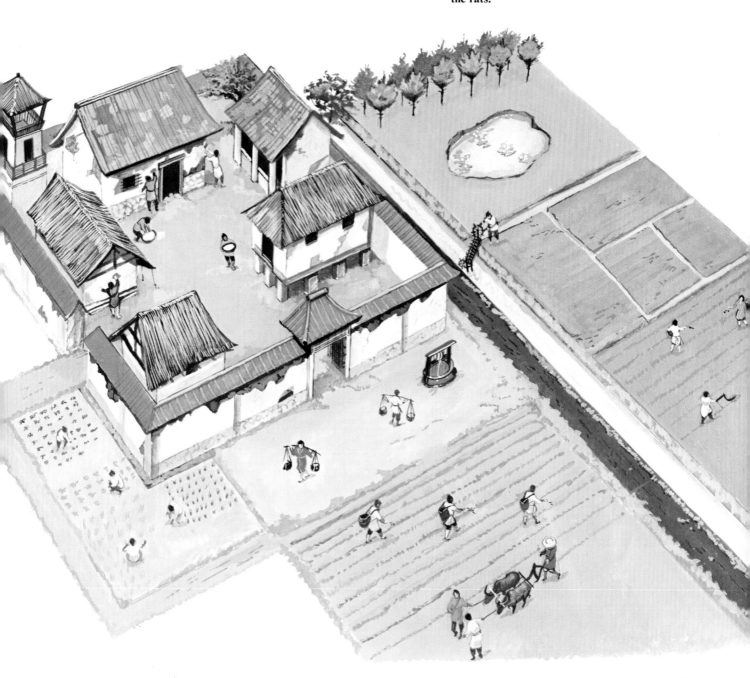

This picture is taken from a stone carving from the time of the Han dynasty (202 BC to AD 221). It shows a man using a spinning wheel at least 1,500 years before James Hargreaves invented the 'spinning jenny' in England. The wheel is being used to spin silk, which was produced in large quantities in ancient China. Orchards of mulberry trees were grown so that silkworms could be fed on their leaves. While the men worked in the fields, the women collected the silk cocoons of the silkworms so that they could be spun. For hundreds of years the Chinese were the only people who knew how to make silk and the secret was jealously guarded. Terrible punishments were threatened for anyone who told foreigners about the silkworm. From Han times on the sale of silk to merchants from the West was the most important link between China and the Near East. Caravans of traders traveled along the Silk Road from Persia and Syria through Turkestan (now in the USSR) and on to China.

The Chinese Inventions

The Chinese are a very gifted race who invented a number of things hundreds of years before any other nation.

The ancient Chinese were not only skilled craftsmen. They were also ingenious inventors. It is not certain if they were the first to discover gunpowder, but they certainly used it. They were also using stirrups to make horse-riding more efficient centuries before they first appeared in other parts of the world.

Measuring Devices
The Chinese realized how important it was to measure things accurately. They had an *abacus* for counting and invented a *water-clock* to measure time. To record distance traveled they invented a device called a *hodometer*. This was attached to a wheeled vehicle and certain distances were marked using a system of cogs. After every *li* (550 yards or 500 meters) an instrument struck a drum; after every ten *li* another struck a bell.

Earthquakes were common in China so they invented a *seismograph* (a machine for recording tremors). It was attached to the ground and whenever there was an earthquake a vertical pole tilted to trigger a mechanism which indicated the direction of the tremor.

Chinese blacksmiths beating and shaping iron at their workshop. Forging in this manner was not common in ancient China because less brittle objects could be made by casting (see top right). But this method was used for making weapons like swords which had to be thin and sharp.

The most skilled of the Chinese metal craftsmen were the bronze workers who made tools and weapons and all sorts of vessels for food and wine. The bronze was poured into a mold and, when hardened, it was decorated with moldings or covered with lacquer. Lacquer is the sap of a type of oak tree which turns black when it is heated. It becomes very hard when left in a damp place and can be polished to a brilliant shine. Pigments can be added to color it. Lacquer was painted on wood and cloth as well as bronze.

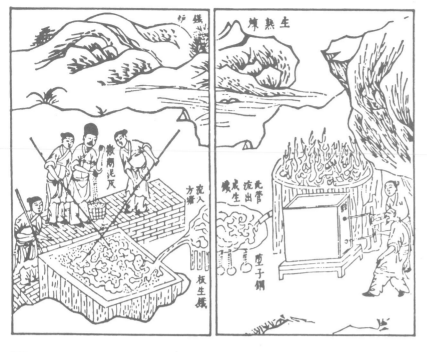

Two of the main industries of the Chinese Empire were the production of iron and salt.

Top: Two men operate large piston bellows which increase the heat in the blast furnaces where the iron ore is melted. The molten ore then pours into a container where it is stirred or 'puddled'. This helps to burn off carbon impurities which would otherwise make the iron brittle. When the iron becomes spongy it is poured into molds. This method of casting iron was much more common in ancient China than forging although it was to be another 1,800 years before cast iron was made in Europe. The production of iron tools made farming in China much more efficient than it was elsewhere.

Bottom: Workers use bamboo tube buckets to raise salt crystals from the mines. Salt was also extracted from saltwater (brine) wells. The brine was collected in iron pans and heated over furnaces until all the water had boiled away and only the salt crystals were left. Salt was important for the Chinese with their grain-based diet, and it was strictly controlled by the government. People had to have a licence for salt production and all selling was controlled by the government.

Below: A T'ang dynasty pottery figure showing a camel laden with Chinese goods for trading abroad. Pottery was one of the first crafts of ancient China. In the early period most pottery was made simply for everyday use, but later in the Han and T'ang periods purely decorative objects were made. The finest of all Chinese pottery was porcelain. Made of a special type of white clay, it can be wafer thin. Porcelain was first made in large quantities during the T'ang dynasty in the 7th century. It was exported far and wide and was highly prized. Indeed the pottery of China had such influence all over the world that the name 'china' is used today for all sorts of pottery and porcelain.

Paper-making

Paper was one of the great discoveries of the Han dynasty. The principle used 2,000 years ago has not changed very much to this day, though we now use different raw materials. The Chinese used mulberry bark, old silk or hemp, which was plentiful, so that their paper was cheap.

The process began by collecting the raw material and mixing it with water. This was trodden to make a sort of paste and mixed with potash. This was then steamed over a furnace and pulped. The mixture was put in a bath of clear water and meshed frames were dipped into it. When the mixture covering the frames had been dried in the sun, there was a sheet of paper.

For a country that was governed so closely, paper was of immense importance. It enabled the Emperor's officials to keep records on which the taxes were based.

Above: Ancient Egypt flourished on the banks of the Nile. Beyond lay desert. The people used a form of picture-writing, or hieroglyphs, shown here.

Below: Some of the treasures which were found in the tomb of the pharaoh Tutankhamun, who reigned in the 1300s BC.

Ancient Egypt

The Egyptians could not have lived without the river Nile. It made the desert lands green and fertile.

The Egyptians could not imagine a world without the river Nile. Every year the river flooded, leaving a fertile black mud on the land. This made it possible to grow wheat and barley, vines, fruit and, vegetables. The people were able to keep cattle and goats for meat and milk. They kept oxen to pull plows, and donkeys to carry sacks of grain and other heavy loads.

The Egyptians used simple machines. They used a *shaduf*, a bucket on a pivoted pole, to lift water out of the Nile and pour it into ditches to irrigate their fields. Besides water, the Nile provided reeds for making ropes, boats, and huts. There were plenty of fish too, and boats could sail up and down the length of Egypt.

Lives of Luxury and Lives of Toil

Wealthy people in ancient Egypt lived in houses built of wood and clay, with decorated walls and fine furniture. Outside there were gardens and ornamental ponds. At a banquet the guests wore gar-

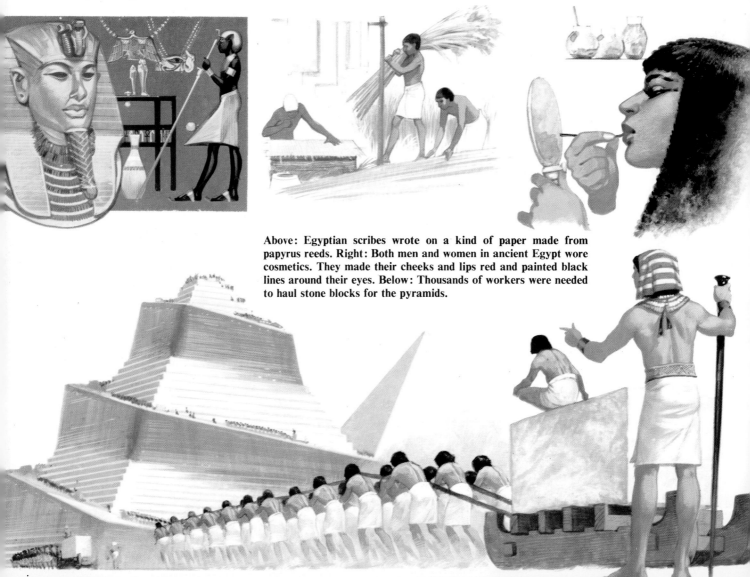

Above: Egyptian scribes wrote on a kind of paper made from papyrus reeds. Right: Both men and women in ancient Egypt wore cosmetics. They made their cheeks and lips red and painted black lines around their eyes. Below: Thousands of workers were needed to haul stone blocks for the pyramids.

Each year between July and October the Nile flooded. The fertile land could then be plowed and sown.

Below: The Egyptians had many gods. Some had the form of birds or animals.

Osiris Amun Anubis Hathor
Horus

lands of flowers around their necks and cones of perfumed oil on their heads. The cones melted slowly and kept them cool.

The peasants lived in mud and reed huts. They slept on bundles of straw. Like everyone else, they had to obey the commands of the pharaohs, or kings.

Mighty Pyramids

Thousands of workers toiled in the sun to build temples to the Egyptian gods and huge stone pyramid tombs for the pharaohs. The later pharaohs were buried in gold coffins, surrounded by things they would need in the world of the dead.

Today in museums you can see the ornaments, tomb paintings, and mummies (preserved bodies) of long-dead pharaohs. In the Nile Valley, temples and pyramids built thousands of years ago still stand. The civilization of ancient Egypt lasted more than 3,000 years, until it was conquered by the Romans.

Below: In war, the Egyptians used fast, two-wheeled chariots. Each chariot carried a driver and an archer or spearman.

The harvesting of wheat by the banks of the Nile was done in March and April each year. The wheat in the fields is being cut with sickles (sharp curved blades on short handles). The wheat is then loaded into baskets and carried to the threshing floor. There oxen trample the grain from the straw stems. The straw is removed with pitchforks. The grain then has to be separated from the chaff (the outer husk). This is done by winnowing. The wheat is tossed in the air. The lighter chaff blows away, while the heavier grain falls to the ground. The grain is then collected in baskets. These are counted by royal officials. The pharaohs always took for themselves a part of all that was produced in Egypt. Once this check has been made, the grain is loaded on to donkeys and taken to the granaries. Notice the water channels leading from the river. Water was of great importance to all Egyptian farmers.

Farming by the Nile

On the fertile land of the Nile valley farmers could grow abundant crops. The villagers on the banks of the river built ditches and dams to control the annual floods. Their wealth led to the development of a brilliant civilization.

The whole of Egypt was first united under a king called Menes in 3100 BC. He built a new capital at Memphis. During the next few centuries the people of Egypt became more skilled in copper-smelting and stone masonry. The first monument built entirely of cut stone was constructed. This was the famous step pyramid of King Zoser at Saqqara.

The Pharaohs

The Pharaohs were not only kings. They were also war leaders and gods. They owned all the land and farmers had to give them part of all they produced. Officials fixed the exact amount due each year. For part of the year the farmers worked on royal projects such as building pyramids or new irrigation ditches.

In spite of two civil wars and numerous foreign invasions, Egypt under the Pharaohs flourished for nearly 2,000 years. Under Thutmosis III (1504-1450 BC), Egypt controlled Palestine and Syria, and the state of Nubia in the south.

As the centuries passed famines and wars made Egypt weak. By 1100 BC it was surrounded by powerful enemies and within fifty years peoples from the West (in what is now Libya) had seized the throne. For a short time the Egyptians regained control of their own land, but in 341 BC the Persians invaded. They were followed by the Greeks under Alexander the Great, and finally, in 31 BC, Queen Cleopatra was defeated by the Romans at the battle of Actium.

Trade by Land and Sea

During the years of plenty Egyptians traded widely around the Mediterranean. Surplus corn, gold from Nubia, as well as copper and building stone were exchanged for materials Egypt lacked. In return for linen and stone vases, Crete sent timber, wool and finely decorated pottery. In the later period horses came from Syria. Trade routes were protected by forts, and Egypt's strong navy.

Clothes and Jewelry

When working in the fields or building pyramids and canals, the Egyptian peasant men and women wore little because of the great heat. Usually, they wore only a short skirt and sandals. After the day's work, the men would change into a long skirt reaching to the knees or ankles. Women wore a dress or tunic held in place with two straps. Pharaohs wore pleated skirts of linen. Over this they tied a leather belt inlaid with precious stones.

Well-to-do Egyptians wore a lot of make-up. They used eye-paint and made lipstick from crushed red ochre mixed with oil. There were many hair styles. Some had plaits, others curls, some wore their hair long to the shoulders. Wigs were also popular. For jewelry, the Egyptians used gold, silver, copper, precious stones and shells. They wore necklaces, rings, collars, bracelets, earrings and headbands.

After-Life in Egypt

The Egyptians worshipped a number of different gods, but they all believed that there was life after death. During life they spent a great deal of time preparing for the next world.

The Egyptians believed that when they died they would be ferried across a river to the kingdom of Osiris, the god of the dead. Osiris sat in judgement while the dead person's heart was weighed against the Feather of Truth. A bad man would have a heavy sinful heart which would outweigh the feather. He would be eaten by a terrifying monster. A good man with a light heart would be taken to heaven by another god, Horus.

So that they could make the journey, it was important that the bodies of the dead should be preserved. The poor were covered in a kind of black tar to seal their bodies from the air. The bodies of the rich were preserved with spices and wrapped in linen cloths as 'mummies'. Pharaohs were placed in coffins. Sometimes there were as many as four coffins, one inside another. They were then placed in a tomb inside a pyramid on the edge of the desert.

The Pharaoh in his official robes.

The Pyramids

The pyramids were built by slaves brought from Nubia and by the ordinary people. A foundation of stones was laid first. Then earth ramps were built to get the stones to the next level. Slaves had to pull the extremely heavy stones on sledges to each level. It was hard and tiring work, especially in the desert sun. The Great Pyramid of Cheops probably took over twenty years to build. It is made up of more than two million blocks of stone. To guard the pyramid a Sphinx was sometimes built outside. This huge sculpture had the face of the dead Pharaoh and the body of a lioness.

The Burial Chambers

Burial chambers in the pyramids could only be reached along a series of complicated secret passages. The Pharaohs had good reason to fear that thieves might rob their tombs, for the burial chambers of kings were filled with jewelry and precious objects. The dead man would need his possessions in the next world so they were buried with him. There was also furniture, food and drink, and instructions for the difficult journey that lay ahead.

The Valley of the Kings

Over the centuries most of the pyramids *were* plundered by robbers who stole everything of value from them. In an attempt to stop this happening many tombs were cut into the cliffs at a place near Luxor. This was called the Valley of the Kings. Again, most of these tombs were eventually discovered by thieves, but one remained undisturbed until it was uncovered in 1922 by two British archaeologists. This was the tomb of Tutankhamun, who lived in the 14th century BC. In his burial chamber were over 60,000 objects, many of them immensely valuable pieces of gold and silver studded with gems.

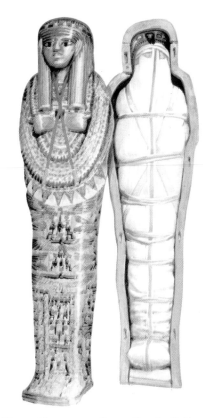

Above: To preserve them after death for the next life the bodies of Pharaohs, priests and rich men were wrapped tightly in criss-crossed strips of linen cloth. Masks of their faces were sometimes also made out of beaten gold or silver.

Left: All the possessions that a Pharaoh might need after death were taken with him to his burial place. Here a long procession of slaves is making its way to a pyramid in the desert. The slaves carry furniture, jewelry and precious objects, as well as food and drink for the dead man. The mummified body already wears a death mask. It has been placed on a boat which is drawn on a sledge. The boat will also be buried with the Pharaoh so that his soul can cross the River of Death to the next world. Alongside the dead Pharaoh march priests who will supervise the actual burial. They carry emblems of the gods worshiped by the dead man as well as offerings to those gods. When the procession reaches the pyramid only the priests and some slaves carrying the Pharaoh's possessions will be allowed into the burial chamber. Once the chamber has been sealed the slaves will be killed so that only the priests know the way to the chamber. This was done to reduce the chance of thieves being able to discover the tomb, although most of the pyramids were in fact plundered in later years. However, Tutankhamun's tomb in the Valley of the Kings remained undiscovered until 1922.

The Greek World

Many of our modern ideas about art, society, law and government are based on those of the ancient Greeks.

More than 4,000 years ago nomadic tribes wandered into the lands we now call Greece. They settled in small villages in the valleys. They were farmers, but the land was not very fertile. So they had to work hard.

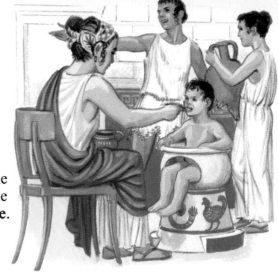

Both men and women in ancient Greece wore a loose tunic called a *chiton*.

Above: King Minos's palace at Knossos on Crete, 4,000 years ago.

Greek Theater

The Greeks built large, open-air theaters, where actors, wearing huge masks performed in plays. The masks told the audience what parts the actors were playing. Actors playing tragic parts wore masks with sad expressions. For a funny part, an actor put on a mask with a smiling face. Female roles were played by men wearing masks with women's faces.

Democracy in Greece

The citizens of Athens liked to read poetry, play music, and discuss ideas.

Below: Theater began in Greece. Plays by great Greek playwrights are still performed, sometimes in ancient theaters that are still standing.

Athens and Sparta

Greece has many mountains, so people could not travel easily. As a result, each city became a separate state. The two most powerful city-states were Athens and Sparta.

The people of Athens liked arts and music. Athenian craftsmen made beautiful vases, jewelry, and statues. The city was full of elegant buildings.

Sparta was very different. The men spent their time training for war. They had few fine buildings or poets.

Greek pottery was decorated, often with pictures of gods and heroes, and stories from ancient legends.

Above: The phalanx was a solid block of *hoplites*, or spearmen. Marching shoulder to shoulder with their spear points bristling, they were a match for any foe.

ALEXANDER THE GREAT
Alexander the Great (356-323 BC) was one of the greatest generals of all time. He became king of Greece after his father, Philip of Macedon, had conquered the city-states and united Greece. Alexander built his empire in only thirteen years.

Below: The empire of Alexander the Great stretched from Greece east to the Indus River.

They also liked to argue about politics. They developed the idea of *democracy*, a government in which the citizens have the right to help make decisions. In ancient Greece only male citizens had the right to vote. Women were considered citizens without political rights. Slaves and non-Greeks were not citizens.

Traders and Athletes
When enemies from outside Greece attacked the country, the city-states banded together to drive them out. The Greeks were also skillful sailors and merchants. They traveled in wooden boats propelled by oars, and traded in ports around the Mediterranean.

The Greeks also enjoyed sport. They set up the Olympic Games in 776 BC. Our modern Olympics are based on the original Greek Games.

GREECE
ASIA MINOR
SYRIA
R. Tigris
R. Euphrates
PERSIA
Mediterranean Sea
R. Indus
EGYPT
INDIA
R. Nile
Border of
Alexander's empire

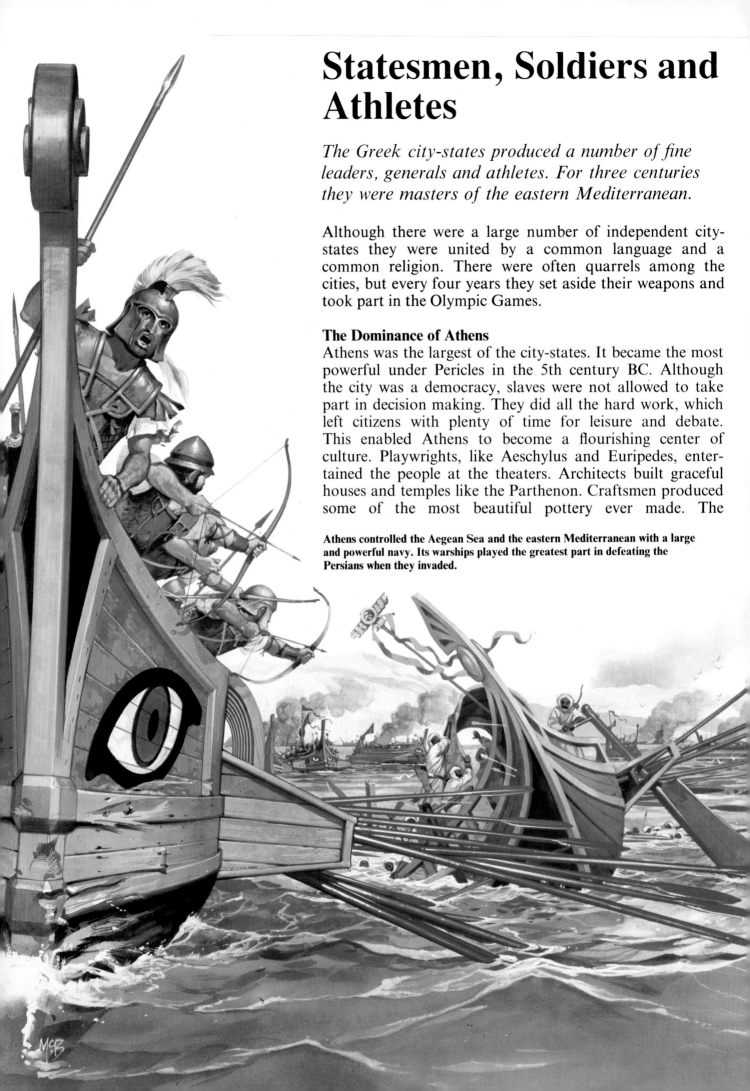

Statesmen, Soldiers and Athletes

The Greek city-states produced a number of fine leaders, generals and athletes. For three centuries they were masters of the eastern Mediterranean.

Although there were a large number of independent city-states they were united by a common language and a common religion. There were often quarrels among the cities, but every four years they set aside their weapons and took part in the Olympic Games.

The Dominance of Athens

Athens was the largest of the city-states. It became the most powerful under Pericles in the 5th century BC. Although the city was a democracy, slaves were not allowed to take part in decision making. They did all the hard work, which left citizens with plenty of time for leisure and debate. This enabled Athens to become a flourishing center of culture. Playwrights, like Aeschylus and Euripedes, entertained the people at the theaters. Architects built graceful houses and temples like the Parthenon. Craftsmen produced some of the most beautiful pottery ever made. The

Athens controlled the Aegean Sea and the eastern Mediterranean with a large and powerful navy. Its warships played the greatest part in defeating the Persians when they invaded.

GREECE IN THE 5TH CENTURY BC

The map shows some of the larger city-states which grew up in the mountainous peninsula of Greece. By the fifth century BC Athens had come to dominate all the rest under the leadership of Pericles (right). He was a brilliant speaker and leader who was elected general in 454 BC in the war against Sparta. Having defeated the enemy, Pericles set about restoring Athens to its former glory. He rebuilt the Acropolis, which was the architectural pride of the city. He became so popular that he was re-elected general every year from 445 to his death in 429. His enemies accused him of wanting to become a dictator, but in truth Pericles was a staunch defender of democracy and he convinced the Assembly of his loyalty to the people.

supremacy of Athens caused great envy among the Spartans. In a war lasting 27 years (described by the historian, Thucydides) Sparta eventually overwhelmed the Athenians.

Greece after Alexander the Great

In their turn, the Spartans were defeated by a king from the north, called Philip of Macedon. His son, Alexander the Great, won a huge empire, which opened up the riches of the Middle East and led to increased trade.

Alexander died young and his successors could not match his great abilities. But Greece remained powerful until Philip V of Macedon foolishly sided with Hannibal against the Romans in 215 BC. They were defeated and the Romans took over lands that had belonged to Greece.

Gods and Goddesses

The Greeks believed in a large family of gods and goddesses who lived together as a family on Mount Olympus. Zeus was the mightiest god because he possessed the thunderbolt. Poseidon, his brother, was lord of the sea, and Hades ruled the Underworld. The goddess of wisdom was Athene, who was also the patroness of Athens. Apollo was god of poetry and the arts. There was a temple to him at Delphi where people went to find out what the future held for them. Apollo spoke through his priestess, the Pythia, and his answers could usually be interpreted in different ways.

Everyday Life in Athens

After a light breakfast Greek men might visit the Agora (the market place) to discuss business. Then they would go to the gymnasium to exercise and have a bath. In the late morning they might visit the Assembly to listen to debates about how the state should be ruled. All this time the women would be at home supervising household duties, which would be performed by slaves. Young boys would be at school, where they learned how to read and write and play musical instruments.

In the evening a family would come together for the main meal, which usually consisted of bread, fish, olives and dried figs, washed down with wine or goat's milk.

THE OLYMPIC GAMES

A very important event in ancient Greece was the games that were held every four years at Olympia in northern Greece. Our modern Olympic Games are modeled on these old Greek games.

The most important contest was the pentathlon, a combination of five events. These were a foot race, the long jump, javelin-throwing, discus-throwing and wrestling. Each competitor had to take part in all five events.

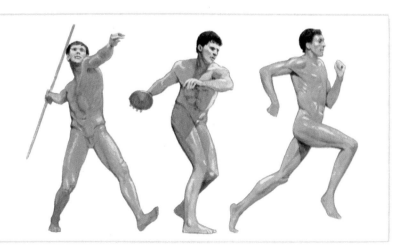

The Roman Empire

The Roman Empire covered most of Europe. It lasted longer than any other empire the world has known. It was won for Rome by the Roman army, which was the best fighting force of its time. For long periods the Empire enjoyed peace. But in many ways it was like a huge armed camp.

The Empire at the time of the Emperor Trajan in the 2nd century AD.

Below: Lictors (attendants) escort a returning Roman general entering the city in triumph. He is wearing a laurel wreath, the sign of victory. He is greeted by crowds of cheering citizens.

Rome began as a small kingdom. It grew first into a republic, and then later into a mighty empire. The emperors ruled over vast lands with the help of the army.

The Roman Empire had much to offer people who lived within its borders. There were well-built roads on which merchants could travel without fear. Aqueducts brought fresh water to the towns; drainage systems kept streets and houses clean. There were laws to ensure peace and safety.

Everyday Life in Rome

Rome was the center of the Empire. Rich Romans lived in elegant country houses. They had baths, central heating, fine gardens and orchards.

The people dressed in *togas*, or robes. They went to the theater and to parties, where they listened to music and poetry. At splendid public baths people could relax in steam rooms and be massaged with sweet-smelling oils.

Gladiators and Slaves

The rich lived comfortably because many slaves worked for them—on farms, in mines, or as household servants. Slaves were punished harshly if they disobeyed.

Within the circus arena armed gladiators fought to the death in front of cheering crowds. The early Christians were punished for their beliefs by the Romans. Some were killed by lions in the arena for the 'entertainment' of audiences.

Guardians of the Empire

Life was often hard and dangerous for the soldiers who guarded the Empire's borders. In forts and camps in Britain, North Africa, and Germany the Roman army stood guard. Every forest, hill, and valley might hold a band of barbarians waiting to attack. In AD 9, barbarians killed 16,000 Roman solders near the river Rhine.

Without its soldiers the Roman Empire would not have lasted so long. But gradually it grew weak. In the AD 400s the army could not guard the frontiers any more. The barbarians invaded, and the Roman Empire came to an end.

javelins

helmet

pickaxe

shield

mess tin

Above: The Roman army was màde up mainly of foot-soldiers. They were divided into legions of about 5,000 men. Each legionary carried his own weapons and supplies on the long marches to the frontiers of the Empire. He was a tough and well-drilled fighter.

Below: Open-air shops used very modern-looking scales to weigh goods such as grain, which were kept in the round basins set into the top of the counter.

To carry water over rivers and valleys the Romans constructed aqueducts. These were bridges supporting a channel along which the water flowed. Here, workmen are lifting blocks of stone into position using a sort of wooden crane. Masons in the background are shaping stone, and carpenters are preparing planks and ladders. A special semi-circular piece of scaffolding is being built for the arches. Perhaps the most important people at work are the surveyors in the foreground. They are plotting the next part of the aqueduct's course.

Great Builders

Throughout their vast empire Romans used their skills as engineers and builders to construct walls, bridges, roads, temples and arenas. Much of their work has survived to this day.

The Roman Empire survived for 400 years against the constant attacks of barbarian hordes because its army was well organized and because it was cleverly knitted together by roads and defensive works. Roads were especially important because armies could move quickly along them to any part of the Empire. They were usually constructed by digging a trench that was then filled with stones and gravel. The surface was paved or cobbled.

This is one of the Romans' most impressive building feats, which has survived for 2,000 years. It is the Pont du Gard in southern France, which was an aqueduct built with three rows of arches. Aqueducts were built to bring water direct from the mountain source to new towns built in the valleys. Water was needed, not only for drinking, but also for the public baths which were so important for the Romans. Both men and women visited the baths at least once a day. They could swim in the heated pools or sit in a steam room before plunging into the *frigidarium*, which was an unheated pool. After bathing, the Romans would be massaged by slaves. They also had their bodies oiled with olive oil which they scraped off with an instrument called a *strigil*. Baths were the great meeting places where friends could relax and chat together.

Roman Towns

Within their walls, towns were carefully laid out on a grid system. Along the streets there were houses and workshops for craftsmen. The town's main streets led from the gates and met at the center of the town, which was the *forum*. This was a spacious open-air meeting place surrounded by covered markets, temples, council chambers and a large hall called the *basilica*. In one part of the town there was usually a barracks where soldiers stayed until called out to a nearby trouble spot. Some of the soldiers patrolled the walls and guarded the main gates.

Roman Villas

Villas were large airy houses set in lovely gardens. Floors in villas were often decorated with mosaics (small colored stones set together to produce a decorative design). Villas were heated by underfloor pipes.

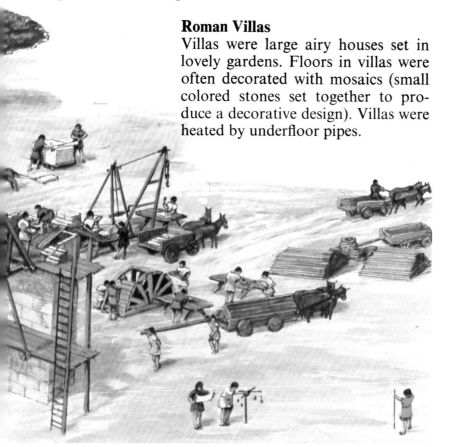

Life in the City

Rome was the heart of the Empire. Built around seven hills on the banks of the river Tiber it had a population of about 1.5 million people in the reign of the Emperor Hadrian (AD 117–138).

As the Roman Empire grew, so too did its capital city. Victories in distant lands brought great riches and this was reflected in the grand buildings and monuments of the city. Particularly splendid were the senate chamber, the temples and the government buildings. Following a series of conquests the Emperor Trajan rebuilt much of the area around the forum, adding a new covered market that was four stories high. He also built a column 125 feet high on which a spiral carving, winding from the top to the bottom, depicted all his victories.

Where People Lived
About a third of the population lived in one-family houses. Everyone else lived in crowded blocks of apartments. These were often unsafe and frequently fell down. Fires were

A view of the forum in Rome today. Considering its age, the fact that so much has survived is remarkable. In the foreground are the remains of the Temple of Vesta. Behind it is the arch of the Emperor Septimus Severus. Such arches were built to commemorate famous victories. In the background on the left-hand side is part of the Colosseum.

also common. The streets were usually dark and narrow and covered with filth of every kind. Few people went out after sunset for fear of being attacked and robbed in the dark. At night it was common to hear the noisy trundling of ox-carts along the cobbled streets, for no wheeled vehicles were allowed to use the streets by day.

How Rome was Governed

The Senate ruled the city and the Empire. It was supposed to be elected by the people, but at different times it was often made up of people who had managed to buy their office. In the early days there were many bloody disputes between the Senate and the people who thought they were not being properly represented. When Julius Caesar came to power he controlled the Senate by tripling the number of its members. The old guard, afraid that Caesar might attempt to make himself king, assassinated him.

After the civil war which followed, Caesar's heir, Octavian, emerged the victor and made himself Emperor. Under his successors the Senate's power declined. Men chosen by the Emperor ruled the city and the Empire. The most important of these was the Prefect of the Praetorian Guard who controlled the army in Italy and could demand taxes to pay for its supplies.

Top: This is how an artist imagines the Colosseum would have looked. Built in the first century AD, the arena was used mostly for bloodthirsty gladiatorial combats. 50,000 Romans could sit in the four rows of terraced steps and watch the terrible spectacles.

Above: Chariot racing was the most popular sport in Rome. A quarter of a million people could cram into Rome's largest stadium, the Circus Maximus. Driving a chariot was extremely dangerous and required great skill. The chariots could easily topple over on the bends. The driver then could be dragged along the ground, or be trampled on by the following horses. But the races provided a good opportunity for placing bets.

Great Religions

Religions began when people realized that there were forces in the world that they could not explain. Such forces, they believed, must be controlled by all-powerful gods.

Three Great Religions
Judaism, Christianity, and Islam all arose in the Middle East. Each teaches belief in one God instead of many gods. And they are all interested in the bond between God and people.

Judaism
The oldest of the three religions is Judaism. It began some 4,000 years ago. Abraham, leader of the Hebrews, a desert tribe, taught his people to worship one god instead of idols and spirits. About 500 years later the Hebrews moved into Egypt to escape famine. In time they were made slaves by the Egyptian pharaohs. They were rescued by another great leader, Moses, who led them out of Egypt.

On their journey back to Canaan, on the eastern shore of the Mediterranean, the Hebrews, later known as the Jews, wandered for many years in the Sinai Desert. According to the Bible, Moses climbed Mount Sinai, where God gave him two stone tablets on which were written the Ten Commandments (laws) for the people to obey. When the Hebrews reached Canaan they tried to live by the laws of their God.

Above: The Old Testament tells how God spoke to Moses from a burning bush, and told him to lead the Hebrews out of Egypt into the Promised Land.

Below: Jesus carried his message of God's love to people in many parts of Palestine.

Romans tried to stop them. They spread his teachings all through the Roman Empire. Many Christians were killed by the Romans for their faith. But 300 years after the death of Jesus, Christianity was made the religion of the Roman Empire.

Islam

While Jesus was preaching, the desert tribes of Arabia continued to pray to idols and spirits. About AD 600 an Arab named Muhammad set out to teach his people to worship one God. He proclaimed himself the prophet of Allah, the true God, and began to teach *Islam* (submission, or obedience, to the one true God).

Worshipers of the old gods drove Muhammad out of Mecca, his birthplace. In 622 he fled to Medina, where he gained many followers. In 630 he returned to Mecca with an army. The Muslims (followers of Islam) captured Mecca and destroyed the old idols. Muhammad died in 632. By then all Arabia was Muslim. After a century of holy wars, Islam had spread from Spain to India.

The Jews look forward to the arrival of a great leader, the Messiah, who will bring peace and love to the world.

Christianity

In 63 BC the Romans conquered the Jews. Some Jews wanted to fight the Romans. Others thought that the long-promised Messiah would save them. Some Jews thought that Jesus of Nazareth was the Messiah. He preached that he was the son of God and the saviour of mankind. He taught that God would reward the humble and gentle with everlasting happiness in heaven. But to some people Jesus was just a troublemaker. The Romans agreed, and Jesus was put to death by a Roman form of execution, crucifixion.

Jesus's followers, known as Christians, went on practicing his teachings, although the Jews and later the

Top: The Muslims waged war to spread Islam. Their cry was 'The Koran (the Muslim holy book) or the sword!' They built splendid mosques all over the Muslim world. Above is the Blue Mosque in Istanbul, Turkey.

THE RELIGIONS OF ASIA

About 500 years before the birth of Christ, the great religious teachers Confucius and Lao Tse lived in China, and Siddhartha Gautama (Buddha) lived in India. The religions they founded are called Confucianism, Taoism (founded by Lao Tse) and Buddhism. All these religions are concerned with the search for truth. They teach ways of living a good life.

Hinduism, the traditional religion of India, is a much older religion. Its beginnings go back as far as 2500 BC. Over thousands of years, early Hindu teachings developed into a very complicated system. The teachings tell people the way that they should lead their lives. A Hindu believes that if he lives correctly in this lifetime, he will be born again at a higher level in the next. According to Hinduism, many lifetimes must be lived on Earth before a person can fully understand the great truths of the universe.

Invaders from the North

For over 250 years much of western Europe suffered from raids by fierce men from Scandinavia. These were the Vikings whose great skill enabled them to cross treacherous seas and cause havoc wherever they landed.

There were a number of reasons why the Viking invasions should have started at the end of the 8th century. The growth of royal power in Norway and Denmark led many young men to seek an independent life overseas. A large increase in the population had led to a shortage of land, especially for younger sons. At a time when excellent sailing ships had been developed rumors of tempting wealth in Christian churches began to reach the Scandinavian lands. Being pagans, the Vikings had no respect for the sanctity of churches and they knew they would be largely undefended. Priests and monks who wrote histories of these events were horrified that their churches were ransacked. They probably exaggerated the size and ferocity of the attacks.

The Vikings believed that the spirits of important people had to sail to a land of the dead. Kings and chiefs were therefore buried in their ships with all their belongings. In some places the ships were buried in damp clay which preserved the wood in perfect condition. This ship was discovered at Oseberg in Norway. Largely built of oak, it has one central mast from which a single large sail was unfurled. When becalmed, ships such as this could be rowed.

When the Vikings raided foreign lands they normally came in small bands from one or two ships. Large raiding parties, of 400 or so, were rare. The Vikings landed on a deserted stretch of coast and made their way inland at great speed. Their attacks usually took people by surprise. Churches and monasteries were favorite targets because they would contain gold and silver and other valuable objects. The monks who wrote accounts of these attacks probably exaggerated the ravages of the Vikings.

The Vikings in Britain

The Vikings first raided Britain in 793, killing one royal official on the south coast. Four years later the isolated monastery at Lindisfarne, in Northumbria, was sacked. After this, raiders appeared on Britain's shoreline nearly ·every year. Occasionally they settled on offshore islands and returned annually to demand tribute from the defenseless people on the mainland.

In 876, Norwegians settled in York and quickly set up their own kingdom. Meanwhile Danes attacked the south of England. Alfred the Great, king of Wessex, led the resistance to them and, in 886, he defeated their leader, Guthrun. Guthrun agreed to become a Christian and his followers were allowed to settle in eastern England in the area called the 'Danelaw'.

The Vikings in France

Much the same pattern of events happened in France. In the ninth century the Vikings came to plunder or exact tribute almost every year. They even rowed up rivers and attacked great trading centres like Rouen, many miles inland.

In 911 the Franks, who were the rulers of France, decided to allow some of the Vikings under a chief called Rollo to settle in Normandy. They hoped that Rollo would then help to ward off other Viking attacks. The Vikings in Normandy grew rich and prosperous because of the good farming land. Gradually, they took over French customs and the French language. They also became Christians.

Viking Adventurers

Some Normans did not, however, lose their Viking passion for adventure. Some followed Duke William of Normandy on his expedition to England in 1066. Having defeated the British at the battle of Hastings they were given lands in the kingdom.

One family set out for the Mediterranean and conquered the island of Sicily. Other parties took their ships along the rivers deep into Europe. Some ended up as special troops in the Russian army. Others traded in such distant places as Baghdad and Constantinople.

But the longest journeys were across the Atlantic. Iceland, Greenland, Newfoundland and northern Canada were all discovered by the Vikings.

The Norsemen at Home

Farming was the chief occupation of the Vikings. Many of those who went on raids in the summer would return home for the harvest. Though ruthless in raids overseas, the Vikings at home were law-abiding and religious.

Women played a more important role in Viking life than they did in many other societies in the early middle ages. A woman frequently influenced her husband in his affairs and took charge of the farm when he went away on a raid.

The whole family worked on the farm together with the slaves, who were called *thralls*. The fields were planted with wheat, barley, oats and rye, and animals such as sheep, cattle and pigs were reared. In the summer, the cattle were taken up to graze on the mountain pastures and the farmers sometimes camped up there with them. In the autumn the crops were harvested.

Thralls would often perform other tasks. They were sent to burn charcoal, which was needed as fuel in the blacksmith's furnace, or they would cut peat when wood was scarce.

The Viking homes

The Vikings were a very hospitable people and loved to entertain visitors. Traveling craftsmen and traders were made very welcome and often stayed for a while on the farm. The buildings, therefore, had to accommodate large numbers of people. The main building was the long hall, whose roof was supported by two rows of posts down the middle. A large fire was placed in the center of the room. Guests spent the night wrapped in furs beside it. For the main meal everyone sat on benches along the walls. Food was cooked in a separate firehouse and brought into the hall on dishes.

Sagas and Poetry

As a family and their guests sat around the fire after their evening meal they would listen to stories about the life of a great king or the deeds of a famous family. These were the *sagas*—stories learned by heart and handed down from generation to generation. The sagas had to be memorized since the Vikings had no paper. Their only writing was letters carved on wood or stone (*runes*).

Above: A Viking fortress at Trelleborg in Denmark. The building in the middle is a reconstruction of one of the boat-shaped houses in which warriors lived. These soldiers were summoned by the king who sent a 'war arrow' to every house in the area. All men who were shown the war arrow had to obey the call or they were outlawed. In the fortresses they would discuss the forthcoming battle and listen to their leader's plans.

Law and Order

Despite their reputation as a wild and lawless people, the Vikings at home had great respect for order. They believed their kings were descended from gods and they would follow these leaders whenever called upon. At the start of the Viking age there were many kings, but gradually one family in each of the Scandinavian lands of Norway, Sweden and Denmark gained supremacy.

Law operated on a system of compensation. If a murderer was caught by the victim's family, he could be killed legally in revenge. Alternatively, he could be taken to a court, called a *Thing*, where it was decided how much the family should be compensated in silver. A most dreadful punishment was to be outlawed, for that meant that a man would be shunned by the community and stripped of his protection by the law.

Craftsmen

The Vikings are chiefly remembered as master craftsmen of ships. These were built in different ways for different uses. The ship-builders knew exactly what wood should be used for each part and planks were made by splitting tree trunks with wedges. Large sailing ships, like the one which was found buried at Gokstad in Norway, were clinker-built; that is, the sides were made up of overlapping long planks. For their size, ships like this were very light and could make good speed with a following wind. But to survive the rough waves of the Atlantic Ocean and the North Sea they had to be sturdy. Vikings are known to have reached Greenland and America.

Vikings decorated their ships with fine carvings. Often the ends of the bow and stern posts rose up in carved heads of animals and monsters that must have greatly alarmed any enemies encountered at sea.

Gold and silver were highly valued by the Vikings. Most of it came from coins which they seized on raids. These were melted down and shaped, by hammering and casting, into beautiful ornaments. Often jewelry was covered with curved patterns, and many objects were inlaid with silver.

Top and right: A landowner or trader and his wife. We have a good idea of what Norsemen wore since clothes are often described in the sagas. Cloth was imported from abroad and might be trimmed with fur. People loved bright colors and both men and women wore jewelry. Men wore tight trousers and a long-sleeved shirt with a belted tunic over it. Women wore full-length dresses. On top of these were over-garments held by brooches.

The Middle Ages

*After the collapse of the Roman Empire, there followed
a thousand years of confusion, hardship and violent
struggles for power in Europe. These were the centuries
we call the Middle Ages.*

The 'Middle Ages' is what historians call the years between the fall of
Rome in AD 476 and the start of the more peaceful, settled Renaissance
era in the 1400s. When the law and order of the Roman Empire disappeared, the barbarian tribes spread across Europe, killing, destroying,
robbing, and carrying off people as slaves.

In the 400s and 500s people shuddered with terror at the mention of
barbarians like the Goths and Vandals. Consequently, people were so
concerned just with day-to-day survival that there was little time left for
the refinements of life. Art, music, and literature continued to develop but
did not flourish until less dangerous times.

The Feudal System

People in Europe banded together to protect themselves. A way of life
called the 'feudal system' developed. Under this system peasant farmers
swore to work for and obey powerful nobles. In return, the nobles
promised to protect them. In this way the peasants became the obedient
'vassals' of their 'liege lord'.

The nobles became vassals of more powerful leaders, such as dukes or
kings. The nobles promised to provide the ruler with men to fight wars.
In return, the ruler protected the nobles.

The Castle Fortress

The center of feudal life was the castle. The noble and his household
lived inside the castle. The peasants lived outside, and farmed the noble's
land. In times of danger they moved inside the castle for protection.

**Above: The charge of the Norman
knights at the Battle of Hastings,
fought during the Norman invasion of
England led by William the Con-
queror. William introduced the feudal
system into England. He replaced the
English lords with his own nobles.**

Feudalism in Britain

In 1066 William of Normandy invaded England. He brought the feudal system into his newly conquered lands. For many Saxon peasants in England who became vassals of the Norman barons, this meant a life of near-slavery. The peasants were not allowed to gather wood or hunt in certain forests. The barons kept these forests for their own hunting. When the peasants in northern England rebelled, the Normans laid waste almost the whole of the north of England and killed many Saxons.

The Peasants

Life was always hard for the peasants. They worked from dawn to dusk on the lands belonging to their lord, and went home to simple houses built of wood and mud. The nobles also led difficult and dangerous lives. Europe in the Middle Ages was a violent place. Power was in the hands of the strongest, and feudal lords spent a great deal of their time fighting to gain power, to protect themselves, or for their king.

The Power of the Church

Churchmen wrote the documents and histories of the Middle Ages. And they belonged to an organization that was more powerful than that of the nobles.

The pope in Rome, the head of the Church, was like a liege lord with all the Christians of Europe as his vassals. Kings and nobles had power over only their own vassals. But the Church could control the beliefs and conduct of people all over Christian Europe. People believed they were defying God if they opposed the Church.

Below: Outside the castle the peasants farmed the land. A different crop was grown in each field each year. The fields were divided into strips among the peasants. In the castle courtyard a hawking party is setting out. Hunting with birds of prey was a popular sport.

51

Knights in Armor

During the Middle Ages everyone admired and feared the armored knight on horseback. The knight was the 'tank' of the medieval period but he was expected to be more than just a good fighter.

This was the great age of chivalry. The knight was supposed to be brave and noble. Armed with lance, sword, and shield, he rode forth to defend the Church, help the weak, and fight the king's foes.

A boy had to train for years before he could become a knight. First he had to work as a page in the castle of a baron. Later he served as squire to a knight. He had to learn to fight and to serve others before he could become a knight himself.

The Knight in Battle

The early knights had armor made of small round links of iron, called *mail*. Later, they began to wear heavy plate armor on their knees, legs, and shoulders. By 1450 the knight was almost completely covered in a suit of steel armor.

A knight's horse had to be big and strong to carry him, his armor, and his weapons. By the 15th century, even the horses were covered with armor.

Jousting

To train for battle, knights fought in mock battles, or jousts. These fights were friendly but dangerous, even though blunt swords and lances were used.

In the great halls of the nobles' castles, minstrels told stirring tales of brave knights, who fought fierce monsters and rescued ladies from danger.

Above: Two knights jousting at a tournament. Below: From left to right, these mounted knights show how armor developed from chain mail to heavy suits of steel plate.

French armor 1100s

French armor 1200s

English armor 1300s

German armor early 1400s

THE CRUSADES
Between 1096 and 1270 Christian armies set out from Europe to recapture the Holy Land from the Muslims. There were many 'Crusades', as these holy wars were called. The Crusaders were not successful, but they brought a great deal of new knowledge of the East to Europe. The Christian knights who led the Crusades did not show much chivalry towards their enemies. In 1099, when they managed to capture Jerusalem, they slaughtered many Jews and Muslims, including women and children.

Below: The great Muslim leader Saladin whose forces captured Jerusalem in 1187. Richard I of England (below left) led an army to the city, but was unable to recapture it.

Greed and Cruelty

Despite the fine tales, not all knights were brave and chivalrous. Many were cruel, greedy, and unjust. Some joined the Crusades only to get rich and win lands for themselves.

Guns and cannon brought an end to the age of the knight. Heavy armor was no match for cannonballs. In time, knighthood became just an honor, given by the king for valued services.

53

Warfare

Kings fought wars for power and glory and their barons followed them out of loyalty or greed. The ordinary soldier fought for a livelihood or because he was forced to.

Warfare was common in Europe during the middle ages. Kings had to face rebellions from over-mighty barons, or they fought each other for lands. The Hundred Years' War was fought because the kings of England claimed lands in France. To be a famous, courageous knight was the most honorable position a man could attain and ballads were written about heroic deeds. Both Christians and Muslims applauded the fighters in the Crusades who struggled for mastery of the Holy Places.

Methods of Warfare

Warfare changed very little during the Middle Ages. Knights on horseback were considered to be the cream of the army because an effective charge could break up the enemy's lines and cause panic and confusion. But over the years knights became less effective. Heavy plated armor for both knights and horses slowed them down and made them less able to turn quickly. Also, pikemen on the flanks and in the front row of a band of foot soldiers proved an effective deterrent to the cavalry charge.

The Long Bow

For hundreds of years bows and arrows had been used in battle, but it was not until the middle of the 14th century that skilled archers, equipped with the long bow, time and again proved to be decisive. The longbow was usually made of ash or yew and was about six feet in length. It was capable of great accuracy and had tremendous penetrating power. It could pierce armor or four inches of oak. The longbow was largely responsible for the English victories against the French at Poitiers, Crecy and Agincourt.

By comparison, the crossbow, which was much favored in Germany, was slow and unwieldy. Until the invention of guns and cannon the longbow was the most effective weapon in battle.

The invention of cannon was also the death blow for the other main feature of medieval warfare – the castle. No castle wall could withstand the incessant pounding of cannon.

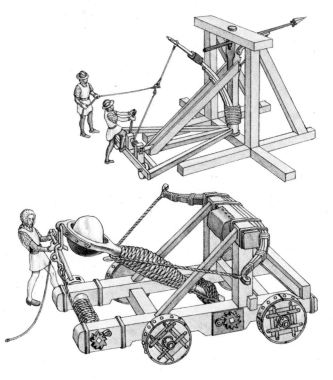

An invading army could not afford to pass a castle without forcing the keepers to surrender. Otherwise its communications could be broken or it could be attacked from the rear. Therefore the castle had to be besieged. The attacking army surrounded the castle and attempted to starve out the defenders. At the same time they tried to take the castle by storm. Siege engines were used like the ones described below. Here you can see soldiers climbing up a siege tower, which was a movable platform built to the height of the walls from which attackers could force their way past the defenders. A battering ram is being used against the gates.

Left: From the middle of the 12th century castles were built in stone with massive walls surrounding inner bailey walls and a stone keep that was usually built high up on a mound. An attacker wishing to take a castle had a formidable task. Moreover, he had to contend with arrows raining down from the walls as well as missiles dropped from the battlements. The overhanging gallery (top right) is called machicolation and provided cover for the defender. To terrorize the defenders there was a machine called a ballista (top left) which hurled javelins 1,000 feet. Mangonels (bottom left) were spoon-shaped catapults that sent stones crashing against the walls. They were smaller than the trebuchet (bottom right) but, being on wheels, were more maneuverable.

Genghis Khan and the Great Invasion

The conquests of the Mongols under Genghis Khan and his successors were of a scope and range never equaled. Their victories were due mainly to the horsemanship of their cavalry.

The Mongol cavalry was the most effective the world has ever seen. Its chief weapons were speed and surprise. Each man had five horses. One was ridden for a day and then rested for four so that the horses were always fresh. This member of the light cavalry is armed with bow and arrow and javelin. His job was to dart in for a quick attack and then withdraw. The heavy cavalry took part in prolonged skirmishes. They were armed with swords, axes, lassos and lances, which ended in hooks used to unseat the enemy. The horses themselves often wore leather armor. Most Mongol cavalry controlled their horses with their feet which left their hands free for fighting. They generally rode in groups of ten and shared their rations of smoked mutton and dried milk. Their favorite tactic was to attack and then pretend to retreat. When the enemy had broken ranks to pursue, they turned and charged again. Sometimes, in the dry steppe country, they set fire to the grass and attacked under cover of the smoke and flames.

The Mongols were a race of nomadic (wandering) herdsmen who lived in the high plateau of central Asia in the area of the vast and rocky Gobi desert. They spent much of their time driving their herds from one pasture to the next in search of better grazing and hunting lands. Often they fought amongst themselves for the best land.

The early life of their greatest leader, Genghis Khan, is shrouded in a mist of legend. Temujin (later Genghis Khan) was probably born in 1167, the son of a tribal chief. By 1206 he had succeeded in uniting all the Mongol tribes and impressed his authority on them. After subduing other neighboring tribes, including the hated Tartars, he invaded the Ch'in Empire in northern China. Having breached the Great Wall, he ravaged the countryside for three years. Peking fell in 1215, but Genghis Khan was then drawn away to campaigns in the West. He appointed governors to rule the conquered lands in his absence.

The ruler in the West was the Shah of Khwarizm. He had been molesting Mongol caravans of traders, and news of this caused Genghis to invade his lands with 250,000 men. The army became expert in siege warfare, having learned a great deal from the Chinese. Cities fell one by one. The beautiful city of Samarkand was left a smouldering ruin. At Merv the entire population was beheaded. At Ugenchi a river was diverted to flood the city. Eventually, they reached the Caucasus mountains. At the Sea of Azov a huge Russian army of 80,000 men was crushed.

Genghis died in 1227 in a hunting accident, but his conquests were continued by his successors.

Genghis Khan's Successors
In 1237–38 the northern Russian states were heavily defeated in a winter campaign. The ancient city of Kiev fell in 1240 and the same year a campaign was launched against Poland and Hungary. Only the death of Genghis' heir, Ogedei, saved Europe in 1241. Thereafter the Mongols turned their attention to China and the Turkish lands. When the Khan Mongke died in 1259, the Mongol Empire split up.

Government and Administration
The people in lands captured by the Mongols were kept weak by constant demands for tribute. Punishments for crimes were harsh, but the Mongols tolerated other people's religions. Much of the day-to-day administration under Genghis Khan was handled by his chief minister, Lu Chu-Tsai, who was Chinese. He was responsible for the collection of taxes and the taking of censuses.

Above: Genghis Khan receives the allegiance of neighboring tribal chiefs at the start of his life as a great warrior. The Khan's tent was the center of the Mongol court as Genghis was constantly on the move. The scribe or writer was a member of the Uighurs who were the only Mongol tribe who had a written language.
Below: The extent of the Mongol Empire at the time of Genghis' death. It stretched from northern China to the Caspian Sea and south to the Indian Ocean.

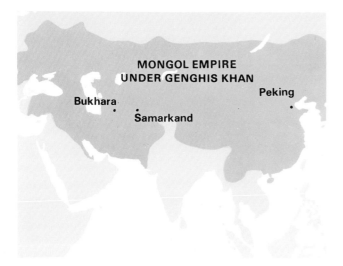

MONGOL EMPIRE
UNDER GENGHIS KHAN

Bukhara
Samarkand
Peking

The Religious Life

Since the earliest days of Christianity people have wanted to escape from the world to pray and devote themselves to God. Some religious people chose to live together in communities.

The people who entered religious communities agreed to live by a set of rules that governed their daily life. These communities were made up of all men or all women. The men were called monks, and lived in monasteries. The women were nuns and lived in convents.

Some of the earliest Christians in Britain lived in monasteries like the one built by St. Columba when he came to the island of Iona, off the coast of Scotland in 563.

Later many British monks agreed to follow a set of rules written by the Italian saint, St. Benedict. These monks were called Benedictines. The monks did not spend all their time praying. They also farmed and studied. Some wrote beautiful books with splendid painted illustrations. Others, like the Venerable Bede, wrote history books.

By the twelfth century, the Benedictines had become very rich. Land was left to them when people died. The monks did less and less work themselves, but hired labor. The monks spent much of their time organizing their large estates.

In 1098, a group of Benedictine monks in France decided to follow a different set of rules. The Cistercians, as they were called, built monasteries in remote places. They did all the work themselves and did not hire servants. A famous Cistercian monastery was at Rievaulx in Yorkshire, England.

The break up of the monasteries

The Cistercians used to graze sheep. When wool became valuable for clothes, they grew rich and, like the Benedictines, they began to employ other people. Many people came to envy them. Henry VIII (1509-1547) decided to close down a large number of monasteries. Their money and land were seized. Many of their fine buildings were destroyed.

Other people had criticized the monks much earlier. In the thirteenth century the followers of St. Francis and St. Dominic decided to travel around the whole time rather than live in monasteries. These friars (or brothers) owned nothing. They begged for their food as they moved from town to town preaching and looking after the poor and the sick.

The most important and largest building in a monastery was the church (1). Here, the monks prayed at various times during the day and at night. They could reach the cloisters (2) from the church. In the cloisters they could read or walk at peace or copy manuscripts.

58

The monks ate twice a day in the refectory (3). It was close to the kitchen (4). The only other room likely to have a fire was the warming room (5). It was probably rather cold where the monks slept in the dormitory (6). Guests would be greeted in the parlor (7). Next to this was the chapter house (8). Here the monks met once a day to listen to the abbot (the head of the monastery) and be told their duties for the day. On the west side of the cloisters were the cellars (9). The food and stores were kept here. Visitors to the monastery would enter by the main gate (10). On one side of this was the almonry (11), where the poor came to receive food and care. Travelers who needed shelter could stay in the guest house (12). Important visitors might go to see the abbot in his house (13), walking across the great court (14). Hay was kept in the barn (15). Bread and beer were made in the brew- and bakehouse (16). Visitors' horses rested in the stables (17). Sick monks were treated in the infirmary (18). Washrooms were usually built over a stream (19).

The Aztecs

The Aztecs, who dominated the northern part of central America during the fifteenth century, were a warlike and cruel race. But they were also great engineers and craftsmen.

The Aztec Empire stretched from the Atlantic to the Pacific coast. The capital, Tenochtitlan, was built on a rocky outcrop in the middle of a swampy lake. Its area was extended by dredging up mud and using it to build platforms. Causeways, wide enough for three horsemen to ride abreast, connected the city with the mainland. Aqueducts brought fresh water to the city. A dike, 10 miles long, protected the city from flooding. At the height of the Empire 1.5 million people lived in Tenochtitlan – no city in Europe at this time was so large.

Emperors, Gods and Sacrifices
The last great Aztec Emperor was Montezuma, who believed that the white man, Cortes, was a god and allowed himself to be taken prisoner by the Spaniards. The Aztec army was later defeated in battle. But Montezuma had been a powerful leader and had made many conquests. He lived in the Royal Palace in the center of the capital. This was a massive two-storied building which also housed the council hall, appeal court, treasury, jail, arsenal and living quarters for 3,000 servants.

Near the Palace was the Temple Precinct, a vast courtyard where human sacrifices were made daily to appease the gods. The Aztecs believed that the sun died each day when it set and that only human blood would revive it. The victims were prisoners of war who went peacefully to their gory deaths because it was an honor to be sacrificed. They would be sent to the Eastern Paradise to live in flower-filled gardens, and after four years their souls would return as humming-birds or butterflies. Being killed in battle was also an honor. All Aztec boys were trained to become tough and brave warriors.

Life on the Swamps
Most of the crops for the citizens of Tenochtitlan were brought from the mainland. But the poor people of the capital had to live from what they could catch or grow in the marshy lake. They grew their crops on plots of land called *chinampas*. These were reed platforms resting on the bottom of the lake. They grew maize, fruit, vegetables and flowers. The houses of these peasant farmers were made of wattle and daub with flat straw roofs. In the one room in each house was a hearth where the staple food of the Aztecs was cooked. This was flat maize pancakes, called *tortillas*. They are still a basic part of Mexican food.

Left: Merchants return to the capital, Tenochtitlan, along one of the causeways linking the city with the mainland. They travel by moonlight. The precious cargoes of jade, jaguar skins and feathers are hidden in the canoes to lessen the risk of being attacked by thieves. They are making their way to the market (above) where produce from all over Mexico is sold. Some of it is unloaded directly from canoes. Rugs, baskets, pots, grain, fish, fruit, beans and other vegetables are all laid out on straw matting. In the background, slaves, with yokes round their necks, have been brought to the market to be sold. One is attempting to escape. If he can reach the Royal Palace he will be freed. In another incident a thief who has been caught is killed on the spot. A court of six sit in judgement on all offenders. The Lord of the Market stands on a dais to make sure that there is fair trading. All goods are exchanged since there is no money.

The market is close to the Palace and the Temple Precinct so processions are common, with the rhythmic sounds of drums and rattles. Women, in brightly colored costumes, dance to the music. Most of the men wear loincloths and capes, since only priests and nobles were allowed to wear more elaborate clothes.

The Incas
of South America

A vast empire grew up in South America in the fifteenth century. Inca warriors defeated other tribes along the western coast but were themselves overthrown by a small band of greedy Spanish conquistadors under Francisco Pizarro.

The conquests of the Inca families based at Cuzco, in what is today southern Peru, did not begin until the reign of their ninth ruler, Pachacuti Inca Yupanqui (1438-1471). With his well trained and well-organized army, he quickly subdued the neighboring tribes. His son, Topa Inca Yupanqui, conquered the Chimu empire to the north. When the next emperor, Huayna Capac, died, the Incas ruled over a belt of land some 2,000 miles long. It was a remarkable achievement.

The Inca army first attacked an enemy from a distance with slings and arrows. Then, in close fighting, they used spears, clubs and swords made of hard wood. They carried shields and wore a form of armor made of heavy quilted material. The emperor would often lead his men into battle. Priests always traveled with the army so that sacrifices could be made to the gods.

Like the Romans centuries before, the Incas built magnificent roads so that their armies could travel quickly through the empire.

Above: A gold plate with a figure representing the Earth goddess, Pacamama, in the center. The Incas worshipped many gods, especially Inti, the Sun god. Left: The emperor leads the ceremonies at one of the great festivals to Inti, held twice a year. The Incas believed that their emperors were descended from the Sun god and for this reason they were obeyed in all things and treated with awe and wonder. Sacrifices played an important part in Inca religion, and a llama was usually killed at the great festivals. Occasionally, humans were also sacrificed.

Right: The Incas grew their crops on hillsides by constructing terraces, which have survived to this day. The soil of each terrace was held in place by a stone wall. Below left: Another example of Inca building. This is Machu Picchu, a fortress built high in the peaks of the Andes mountains.

Administration of the Empire

All the land of the Incas was divided into three parts. Crops grown in one part went to the gods and were used in sacrifices and to feed the priests. Those from the second part went to the emperor and provided food for him, his large family, the army and the officials. The third part was for the peasants, yet matters were so well organized that no family was ever short of food. Llamas and alpacas, which provided wool for clothing, were similarly divided.

The Incas did not have a form of writing, but, by using a piece of string, called a *quipu*, officials could keep records. Other pieces of differently colored string were tied to the quipu and knots were made in them. The colors represented different objects; the knots indicated numbers. Everything in the Inca Empire was counted.

The peasants did not pay taxes to the emperor. Instead, they worked for him in the army or the mines or on some building project for certain lengths of time. This duty was called *mita*.

Crime was severely punished by death, blinding or banishment depending on the offence.

Inca Craftsmen

The Incas encouraged their craftsmen who were provided with food and clothing so that they could practice their skills full-time. Weaving was an ancient craft among the people of the Andes. Cotton grew near the coast and wool was shorn from the mountain animals (llamas, alpacas and vicuna). Many different dyes were used and colorful patterns were woven into the cloth. Feathers and beads were attached to garments for extra effect.

Metalworkers made objects in gold, platinum, copper and bronze. All the mines belonged to the emperor and all the precious metals had to be taken to his capital, Cuzco. He then ordered craftsmen to fashion jewelry, ornaments and models of animals. So many gold objects were made that the Emperor Atahuallpa was able to promise Pizarro a roomful of gold in return for his release when the Spaniards invaded the Inca Empire. Pizarro not only went back on his word and killed Atahuallpa; he also ordered all the gold to be melted down. So all the Inca treasures were lost.

Early Explorers

The people of ancient Egypt and of Greece and Rome knew very little about the world. They believed the Earth to be flat and thought it was surrounded by the ocean. If they sailed too far they might fall over the edge. Once out of sight of land they had no means of navigating except by observing the positions of the sun and stars. But fearless early explorers made some incredible journeys and even discovered America centuries before Columbus.

In 1969-70 a Norwegian called Thor Heyerdahl twice sailed from North Africa to America in boats made from papyrus. He proved that, using the currents and winds correctly, the ancient Egyptians could have crossed the Atlantic.

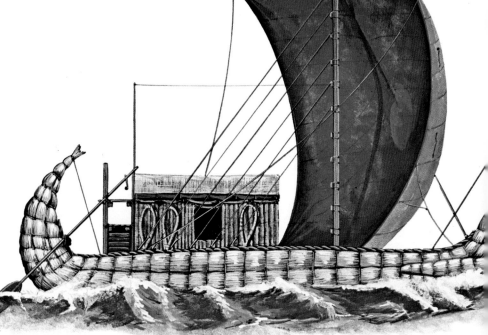

The voyage of Pytheas

Very few Greeks were prepared to sail west beyond the straits of Gibraltar (which they called the Pillars of Hercules) because they feared that they might fall off the edge of the world. But a sailor called Pytheas knew that the Phoenicians had sailed to some islands in the north and returned laden with tin. He determined to make the journey himself and set out with a crew of 40 in a wooden ship with large square sails and oars. Eventually he reached the Tin Islands (which was really Britain) and landed on the coast of Cornwall. Having exchanged the cloths he had brought for the locally mined tin, he decided to continue his journey north. In the record which he kept, he wrote of frozen seas and icebergs. He noted that summer days grew longer and the winter days got shorter as he traveled northward. He was one of the first people to realize that this was a way of discovering how far north you had traveled.

Alexander the Great

Following the death of his father, Alexander had to defend his inheritance against an invasion from the Persians under Darius. Within six years he had conquered Persia and decided to continue his conquests eastwards. He wanted to conquer the world. Leading his army over wild, mountainous country he came eventually to the mysterious land of India. He marched down the fertile plain of the river Indus and defeated the people under their leader, Porus. He continued east, crossing another great river, before his soldiers refused to go any further. They complained that they were too far from home and would not listen to Alexander's pleas that they should continue. They returned by a different route, following the Indus to its mouth and then crossing a vast expanse of desert. Half of the great army died on the way and Alexander himself died of fever at Babylon at the age of 32. But his conquests had opened up the East and

In their carefully designed sailing ships the Vikings made long journeys across the seas. They sailed right round the coasts of Britain and Ireland, and it was a Norseman, Ingof, who first discovered Iceland. Soon over a thousand others from Norway had joined him. One of those who came later was Erik the Red, a man with a fierce temper who had been banished from Norway for killing someone. Soon he was in trouble again for killing another man in Iceland. He decided to set out West. Steering by the stars, he eventually came to a frozen coast with high, snow-covered peaks. This was Greenland.

In 986 an Icelander called Bjarni was driven off course while making his way to Greenland. When the storm died down, Bjarni found himself near a coast. But it was covered with forests and not at all like Greenland. This was the first sighting of America by a European, and, although Bjarni did not land, others later made the journey and settled in Vinland (New-foundland). But after two years these early settlers were driven away by the American Indians. It was 500 years before the next European, Columbus, set foot in America.

merchants soon discovered India was a rich country to trade in.

Ptolemy the Geographer

Ptolemy was a Greek scientist who lived in Alexandria in the 2nd century AD. He was an astronomer who plotted the positions of the stars at different times and at different places. He concluded that the Earth must be round and not flat. Then he guessed, though incorrectly, that its circumference was about 8,000 miles. (It is 24,902 miles.)

Ptolemy was important because he drew fairly accurate maps which were used by explorers for hundreds of years. He also wrote a book called *Geography* which many travelers relied on for more than a thousand years.

The Polos reach China

The greatest explorers in the early middle ages were the Vikings who took their ships deep into Russia and sailed across the Atlantic Ocean. But, meanwhile, other travelers had made great journeys to the East in order to trade and bring back valuable silk and spices.

In the rich trading city of Venice, Nicolo and Maffeo Polo traded in pearls, jewels and silks and made many journeys up the river Volga and into Persia. On one trip they met a caravan of traders who were on their way to the land of Cathay (China). Cathay had been known about for many years but the recent Mongol invasions had so terrified the merchants that few now made the perilous journey. The Polos decided to join the caravan and reached Peking in 1261 where they were welcomed by Kublai Khan (great grandson of Genghis). He asked them to return.

On their second trip to Cathay, Marco Polo accompanied his father and uncle. Their overland journey took three years. Kublai Khan was so impressed with Marco that he persuaded him to stay behind when his uncles were ready to go home. Marco stayed in China for 17 years. He was fascinated by all he saw and kept a diary recording all the places he visited. He described the magnificent buildings and great rivers. He watched the Chinese making silk cloth and printing books—things they had known how to do long before the Europeans. Marco Polo's book was read avidly by the people of Europe on his return. It was an important source of information for future travelers and merchants.

Discovering the New World

Trade with India and the East was important because people needed spices for making their food more interesting, preserving meat and making medicines. But since the great travels of Marco Polo the overland route to India had been blocked by the Turks. A sea route had to be found. Christopher Columbus thought he had reached Asia when he sailed westwards across the Atlantic.

At the beginning of the 15th century most people thought that the only way to reach India by sea was around Africa. A Portuguese prince called Henry the Navigator organized several expeditions down the west coast of Africa, but by his death in 1446 they had only got as far as what is now Sierra Leone. In fact the trip around Africa was not successfully completed until about 27 years later. Even then Bartolomeo Diaz did not realize he had achieved the feat.

Christopher Columbus

Christopher Columbus, a young sailor from Genoa in Italy, was convinced that a route to India could be found by sailing westwards across the Atlantic. Most people thought he was mad, but he managed to persuade Queen Isabella of Spain to put up the money for his expedition.

Columbus set sail from Spain in three ships. The flagship was the *Santa Maria*. It was about 120 feet long and weighed 100 tons. The foremast and main mast were square rigged and the mizzen sail was lateen rigged. The other two ships were much smaller. The *Pinta* was a 50-ton caravel and was captained by Columbus' partner, Martin Pinzon. The *Nina* was only 40 tons. It was captained by Martin's brother, Francisco. The *Santa Maria* was destroyed on rocks near Haiti during a storm, but the two smaller ships managed to get back safely when Columbus returned to Spain.

On August 3, 1492 Columbus set sail from Palos, Spain with 120 men in three ships. After spending a month in the Canary Islands they sailed into the unknown. For a month they had no sight of land and the crew were all for returning home. Then some birds were spotted flying westwards. They knew there must be land nearby. Columbus altered direction slightly and on October 12 the ships found themselves close to a large grass-covered island. Columbus assumed it was an island off Asia and when he landed he called the local people Indians. In fact the island was San Salvador, part of the group of islands we today call the West Indies.

Columbus sailed on and discovered Cuba and Haiti before returning to a hero's welcome in Spain. He made other trips across the Atlantic, still convinced that it would be possible to reach Asia. But in fact he never reached the mainland, which was of course not Asia but the continent of America.

Amerigo Vespucci and John Cabot

America is named after an Italian sailor named Amerigo Vespucci who claimed to discover the 'New World' in a trip which he made in 1497. His stories could not be checked, but if they were correct he reached America three weeks before the Englishman, John Cabot, landed in Nova Scotia in Canada.

When Columbus first landed in the West Indies, he was certain that he was close to the mainland of Asia. He had come to seek gold and to trade with the local people. He also wanted to convert them to Christianity. He therefore carried a cross with him when he landed. He called the people Indians and gave them presents of brightly colored beads and cloths. They were friendly and provided him and his crew with food. But the islands were a disappointment to him because they appeared to have little gold. Columbus decided to report back to Queen Isabella and left some of his crew to settle in Haiti.

On his second voyage he discovered these settlers had been massacred by the local people. Things had not started well and matters got worse. In 1500 there was a rising by some of the Spaniards in the new colony who disliked Columbus' rule. When he imprisoned them, the remaining colonists were infuriated that Spaniards should be treated in this way. Columbus was arrested and shipped back to Spain in chains. He died in 1506 a poor and disillusioned man.

Around the World

The discovery of the New World signaled a new wave of exploratory voyages paid for by European kings, who wanted new lands and trading routes.

Father and son

John Cabot was a sailor and spice merchant who wanted to find a way of getting spices from the East more cheaply than was possible on the overland route. Henry VII, King of England, agreed to finance an expedition to find a sea route to the East. In 1497 Cabot set sail from Bristol, England in his ship, the *Matthew*. After seven weeks he reached Newfoundland. He then sailed south and almost certainly landed in Nova Scotia.

He died before another expedition could be equipped, so his son, Sebastian, went instead. He sailed north from Newfoundland, but the members of his crew were so frightened of the icebergs that they forced him to turn south. He was never able to find the northwest passage to Asia.

Vasco da Gama and India

In the same year as John Cabot's first voyage a Portuguese sailor called Vasco da Gama set out to find a route to India around the coast of Africa. Years before, Diaz had shown that it was possible. Da Gama sailed far out to sea to avoid the dangerous currents of the Gulf of Guinea. He did not see land again for 14 weeks. After nearly four months at sea he rounded the Cape of Good Hope and started northwards. He landed when he reached the coast of what is now Kenya. There one of the local people agreed to pilot him across the ocean to Calicut on the southwest coast of India. After Vasco da Gama's voyage, the way was opened up for other Europeans who set up trading posts all along the Indian coast.

Three of Vasco da Gama's ships on the way to India around Africa. Atlantic storms are common and the little ships were often buffeted mercilessly by the high winds and huge waves. Men were swept overboard in such storms and shipwrecks were not uncommon.

Right: Life on board ships like Magellan's was never comfortable, but in high seas it was also dangerous and frightening. Those who had to be on deck would huddle near any cover to protect themselves from the winds and the icy water that swept over the ship.

Ferdinand Magellan goes round the world

Ferdinand Magellan was the son of a wealthy Portuguese landowner. From an early age he dreamt of finding a route to the Spice Islands of the East by sailing south of the newly discovered America. Unfortunately, he quarreled with the Portuguese king who refused to pay for such an expedition. The King of Spain agreed to support the voyage instead, and on September 20, 1519 Magellan sailed from Seville with a fleet of five ships. Three of these were captained by Spaniards who resented the fact that their commander was a foreigner. Magellan, however, insisted on complete obedience to his orders.

The fleet reached Brazil in December and sailed south to winter in what is now Argentina. The weather was dreadful with two months of gales, mountainous seas and snow. The Spanish captains insisted on turning north. When Magellan refused, they mutinied. In a pitched battle they were defeated and killed.

At last Magellan found the narrow straits leading to the Pacific, but one ship, with much of the stores, had deserted. The remaining ships faced a long journey to the Philippines with little food and many of the crew died. Though members of his expedition eventually got back to Spain, Magellan himself was killed in the Moluccas. But he had achieved his goal of linking the East and the West.

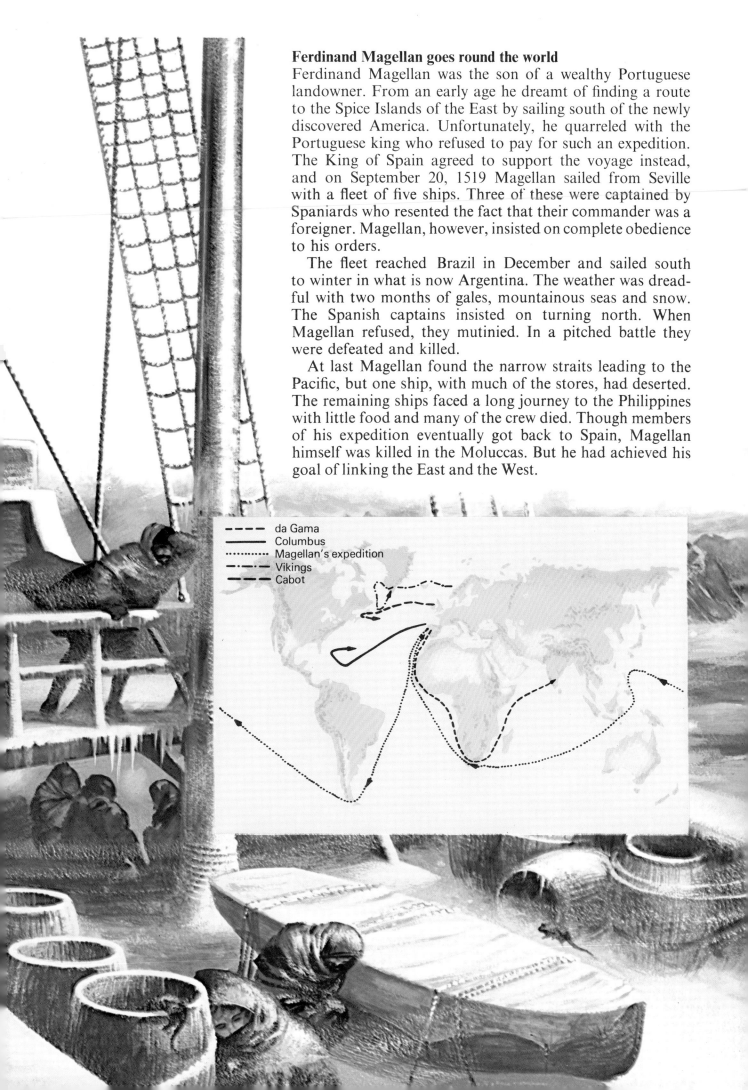

- - - - da Gama
——— Columbus
········· Magellan's expedition
—·—·— Vikings
— — — Cabot

psaltery

lira da braccio
an early bowe[d]
instrument

The Renaissance

The word renaissance means 'rebirth'. It is used to describe the flowering of art and learning in Europe that began in the 1400s. The center of this great movement was Italy.

The New Learning

The Renaissance was a time when men were looking for new ideas. Many of them went back to the ideas of the ancient Greeks and Romans. Great artists, such as Leonardo da Vinci and Michelangelo, followed Greek and Roman examples in their paintings and statues. Architects, such as Bramante, designed buildings with Greek and Roman columns.

During the Renaissance trade flourished. A new kind of wealth—that of rich merchants—appeared. These men were proud of their achievements. They asked artists to paint portraits of them and their families. With this new interest in portraits, painting became more true to life.

The great scholar Erasmus began to study the Bible in a new way, and prepared the ground for fresh thoughts on religion. He believed that people had great abilities that they could use to improve life on Earth.

Top left: Leonardo da Vinci was a painter, sculptor, architect, mathematician, and engineer.

Top: The telescope devised by Galileo.

Above: Musical instruments of the Renaissance.

Right: Michelangelo carved a statue of Moses for Pope Julius II's tomb. Sculptor, painter, architect, and poet, Michelangelo was one of the greatest Renaissance artists.

Science and the Church

Soon more and more people began to study the world around them. They tried to explain what they saw in the heavens. In 1543 a Polish astronomer, Nicolaus Copernicus, suggested that the Earth was round and turned on its axis, and that it moved around the Sun. The Church authorities taught that the Earth did not move. People believed that the Earth was the center of the Universe, and the Sun, Moon, planets and stars moved around it.

The Church did not like the astronomers' ideas because they seemed to contradict the Bible. In the 1500s most people accepted the Bible as an infallible guide not only in religion but in natural science as well. In 1572 a Danish astronomer, Tycho Brahe, saw the 'unchanging' heavens change before his eyes when he saw a star exploding. When the great Italian astronomer Galileo looked at the night sky through his telescope, he saw that Copernicus was right.

Patrons of the Arts

After a time the scholars' love of learning and art influenced the wealthy nobles, princes, and popes. They encouraged artists and architects. They had great palaces and churches built, and filled them with paintings and sculptures. In Rome Michelangelo was employed to paint the ceiling of the Sistine Chapel and design the dome of St. Peter's Basilica.

The ideas of the Renaissance soon spread to France, Spain and northern Europe. The new learning influenced men within the Church itself, who began to question Church authority during a movement called the Reformation. What began as questioning ended in a bitter split. Many people broke away from the Roman Catholic Church to found Protestant Churches.

THE PRINTING PRESS
Until 1440 everything people read had to be copied by hand or printed from hand-carved wood blocks. These methods were very slow, so there were few books, and not many people could read.

Then a German, Johannes Gutenberg, invented movable type that could be used again and again to print different books. This invention helped to spread the Renaissance learning and gradually many more people learned to read and write.

The People of the Renaissance

During the Renaissance there was an enormous leap forward in scholarship and the arts. Trade flourished and ideas blossomed with increased contact between people of different lands.

At the time of the Renaissance, Italy was divided into a number of states. In the North many of these were centered on the great cities like Milan, Genoa, Venice and Florence. Central Italy, including Rome, was ruled by the Popes. The South was ruled by the Kings of Naples. It was in the North that there was the great flowering of art and learning.

The Great Leaders
Some of the most influential political leaders in northern Italy rose to prominence as soldiers of fortune (*condottieri*). There was great rivalry between the different states whose princes wanted ever more land to increase their wealth. Preferring not to risk their own citizens, they hired mercenaries like the Englishman, John Hawkwood, who fought successively for the Pope,

Florence and Milan. Many achieved eminence as a result of their fighting, like Francesco Sforza, who ruled Milan for 16 years, and Federigo da Montefeltro, who became ruler of Urbino.

One family ruled Florence for three generations. They were the Medicis, who were immensely wealthy merchants and successful bankers. Cosimo Medici managed to avoid costly wars and was a great patron of the arts. His grandson, Lorenzo, continued this support and was himself a fine poet.

Popes and Scholars
Though leaders of the Church, the Popes behaved very much like other Italian princes during the Renaissance. They plotted against rivals and fought wars to gain territories. Some led scandalous lives, like Alexander VI, a member of the notorious Borgia family. But they were also passionately interested in the arts. Sixtus IV built the Sistine Chapel in Rome and Julius II often commissioned works of art from Michelangelo and Raphael.

The greatest scholars were known as 'humanists' because they wanted people to take more pride in themselves and the world around them. One of the most famous was Marsilio Ficino who taught Lorenzo de Medici.

Artists, Sculptors and Architects

The two greatest painters of the Renaissance were Michelangelo, who painted the ceiling of the Sistine Chapel, and Raphael, who painted religious portraits more realistically than had been done before. Leonardo da Vinci, who painted the Mona Lisa, spent more of his time on anatomy and engineering. Other great Italian painters were Botticelli, Titian and Uccello.

Some of the great sculptors were Michelangelo, Donatello, Ghiberti and Brunelleschi, who was also an architect.

The Renaissance outside Italy

Great advances were not only made in Italy. In England, the scholars Thomas More and Erasmus were encouraged by Henry VIII who also gave much work to the German painter, Holbein. Other North European painters like van Eyck, Breughel, Bosch and Dürer produced work of exceptional quality. A German called Gutenberg perfected the use of moveable type for printing. This led to the production of more (and cheaper) books. Vesalius, a scientist from Flanders, discovered the importance of anatomy for medicine. A Polish astronomer called Copernicus for the first time suggested that the Earth went around the Sun, not the Sun around the Earth.

These and many more contributed to the great surge in European civilization during the 1400s and 1500s.

The Reformation

The new ideas of the Renaissance and the effects of the voyages of discovery on people's minds led to people questioning many accepted ideas. Even the Catholic Church, which was all-powerful began to be challenged.

There were problems inside the Church. Many of its own rules were broken by bad priests. They grew rich selling 'pardons' for sins. They even sold pardons for the sins of dead people. They sold fake 'relics', too, saying they were hair and bones of saints. People believed these relics would protect them from harm.

This behavior angered the priests who obeyed the rules. Among them was a German priest called Martin Luther. He believed that you could not buy your way into heaven. He thought that the only way to earn God's love was to live a good life. This meant worshipping God in Church and helping other people.

In 1517 Luther posted a list of 95 'theses' (or arguments) to explain why he disapproved of the Church's practices. Other priests in Germany joined in the argument. So too did many German rulers. They wished to weaken the Pope's power over them. Luther himself was excommunicated (driven out of the Church) for his protest. But the protests continued. People began setting up *Protestant* churches.

The Movement Grows

This period when the Church was challenged is known as the Reformation. It has this name because it was then felt by many that the teachings of the Church were changed and reformed.

There were several groups of Protestants. Some followed Luther. Others followed John Calvin of Geneva and other Protestant reformers.

In England, King Henry VIII quarreled with the Pope, when the Catholic Church refused to allow him to divorce Catherine of Aragon. In 1534 Henry broke with the Church in Rome. He closed monasteries and took their land, making himself head of the Church of England. The Anglican and Episcopal Churches grew from this new Church.

Violence and War

The arguments of the Reformation split Christians into two groups: the Protestants, who agreed with Luther and others, and the Roman Catholics, who remained loyal to the Pope and the traditional teachings of the Church.

Both sides, Protestants and Catholics, believed they were right. Neither side was prepared to listen to the ideas of the other. Catholics killed Protestants and Protestants killed Catholics.

One reason for the growth of the Protestant movement

GALILEO'S HERESY
In 1609, the great Italian astronomer, Galileo Galilei, built a telescope and observed the Sun and the stars. He became convinced that Earth moves around the Sun. The Church did not agree. Galileo was accused of heresy and ordered to deny his theory. The story goes that he did deny it, but under his breath said "Yet it *does* move."

was that many rulers were eager to reduce the Pope's power and envied the Church's wealth. So when they heard of Luther's protest, these rulers saw their chance to break away from the Church. They, too, became Protestants.

The argument went on for years. Many nations suffered and the poor people, who hardly entered the argument, often suffered most.

The Effects of the Reformation

The Reformation led to reforms within the Church of Rome. Nevertheless, Protestantism continued to spread. The effects of all this changed the map of Europe. Although the Roman Catholic Church remained as a single Church, the Protestants split up into different groups. Some areas became mainly Protestant and followers of Luther with some Catholic regions; others followed Calvin. Yet others stayed mainly within the Roman Catholic Church with Protestant groups fighting to survive in their midst. The way Europe divided over religion then is largely the way in which it still remains today.

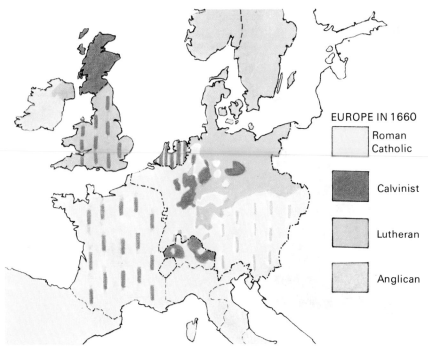

EUROPE IN 1660

Roman Catholic

Calvinist

Lutheran

Anglican

The Reformation changed the map of Europe. The Roman Catholic Church remained a single body, but Protestants were split up into different groups.

PRINTING AND THE REFORMATION
Before the invention of printing, few could read the Bible. There were very few copies and they were written in Greek or Latin. Only the priests could read them. After 1440 when Gutenberg invented the printing press, there were more books. The Bible was translated into English and other languages. People read it for themselves and began to question what the priests told them.

Lefthand page, top: Martin Luther nails his Ninety-Five Theses on the door of the Castle church in Wittenberg, Germany. His theses were written in protest against the sale of 'indulgences' by the Catholic Church to people in search of pardons for their sins.

Right: The Council of Trent, held from 1545 to 1563, made changes in the Roman Catholic Church to strengthen it against Protestantism. This period of reform and rebirth of faith in the Church was called the Counter Reformation.

The Wars of Religion

In the 1600s Europe was ravaged by wars and revolts, largely fought because of religion. Huge armies had set piece battles and generals made their mark with bold new strategies.

Protestantism established itself firmly in most European countries in the second half of the 16th century, due to the reforming zeal of such men as Luther, Zwingli and especially Calvin. But, particularly in France and the Holy Roman Empire, it was only tolerated because the rulers were too weak to challenge it. When they were stronger they attacked the Protestants in their own lands and threatened other countries with Protestant kings. In France, Catholic repression led to the outbreak of over 500 popular uprisings. These continued until 1648 when the largest revolt, the *Fronde*, was put down by Louis XIV. In the Netherlands, Dutch Protestants staged a revolt against their Spanish masters which continued from 1566 to 1648.

In 1618 a war started that was to continue for 30 years. The Holy Roman Emperor defeated the Bohemian Protestants and then attacked the German princes.

The Thirty Years' War

Despite the help given to the German Protestants by England, Denmark and the Dutch, the Emperor had established his superiority by 1629. The Protestants were only saved from collapse by the arrival of military aid from King Gustavus Adolphus of Sweden. The Emperor was defeated at the battles of Breitenfeld (1631) and Lutzen (1632). At Lutzen, Gustavus Adolphus, who had shown himself to be a commander of genius, was opposed by another great general of this period. This was an Austrian mercenary called Count Albrecht von Wallenstein. The Swedes eventually won the battle, but at great cost. Over 5,000 of their men were killed, including Gustavus Adolphus himself, who was shot through the head.

After the battle, Spain entered the war to aid the Emperor. France, keen to see the Emperor humbled, joined the Protestants. All Europe was involved in the war, which lasted until 1648. When the Peace of Westphalia was finally signed, Germany was ravaged and impoverished. The Emperor's domains were split into 234 different territories. Germany was not to recover for 200 years.

King Gustavus Adolphus of Sweden leads his men into battle during the Thirty Years' War. Sweden's intervention in the war was not only crucial for the Protestant cause; it also established Sweden as the greatest military power in Northern Europe. This supremacy was not to be challenged for 75 years until Peter the Great of Russia appeared on the European stage. Gustavus Adolphus was not only an inspiring leader who was always the first in attack, he was also a great innovator in military techniques and strategy. Until his day, pikemen and musketeers had dominated the battle-field. Gustavus concentrated instead on increasing his fire power and its mobility. Musketeers were made more effective by lightening their muskets and giving them paper cartridges which speeded up re-loading on the battlefield. More light mobile guns were introduced to give support. Careful training and planning led to cooperation between infantry, cavalry and artillery. This made it possible for the wedge-shaped Swedish formations to overwhelm the traditional great square formations of massed pikemen and musketeers. The battle of Lutzen in 1632 was a classic example of the new methods of warfare. It brought the brilliant Gustavus into conflict with the other gifted general of the early 17th century, Count Wallenstein.

Sea Power

In the 1500s, rival nations of Europe struggled for control of the sea routes to the New World. The navies of England, France, Spain, and the Netherlands all competed to 'rule the seas'.

The first Europeans to start colonies in America were the Spaniards. They had provided Columbus with the ships that reached America in 1492. Being proud and religious people, the Spaniards came to believe that God had shown them special favor and had 'given' them America. So they did their best to prevent other Europeans from settling there.

The Spaniards' great rivals were the French, Dutch, English, and Portuguese. All of these also wanted territory in the New World. The French and English settled in North America and the Dutch and Portuguese started colonies in South

The English sent eight 'fire ships' into the Spanish Armada. These were filled with gunpowder and set on fire. The Spanish ships were forced out to sea to escape the flames.

America. All of them claimed different islands in the Caribbean Sea.

The English Threat

Of all their rivals, the ones the Spaniards hated most were the English. They had good reason: the English and their queen, Elizabeth I, were determined to have a share in the great riches to be found in America. Great seamen such as Francis Drake thought nothing of crossing the Atlantic with a few ships to raid and plunder the Spanish settlements on the South American coast.

The Armada

The Spanish king, Philip II, decided to punish the English. He sent a huge fleet of 130 ships, the *Armada*, to attack England. At that time, war at sea was fought by soldiers, not sailors. A captain aimed to fasten his ship to an enemy with great iron hooks called grappling irons. Then planks were laid across so that soldiers could run on to the enemy's deck. There the battle was fought.

The Spanish galleons were built for this kind of warfare. They had high sterns and bows, and sides up to five feet thick. There were three times as many soldiers as sailors on board.

When the Armada reached the English Channel, the Spaniards saw that they outnumbered the smaller English ships. They were sure of victory—but they were wrong. The English warships were a new type, built by the great seaman John Hawkins.

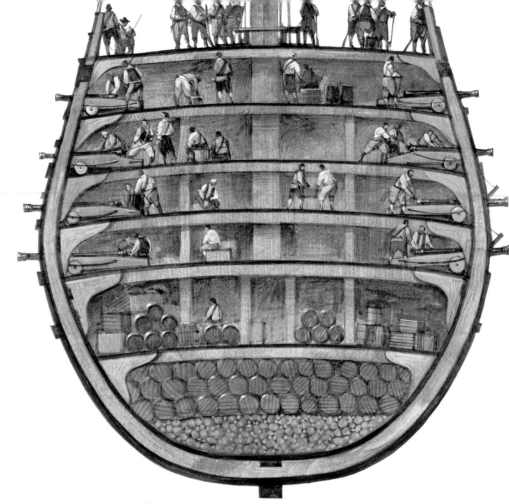

Above: A cross-section of a Spanish galleon, showing the gun decks. Below: Rich Spanish colonies in the West Indies were often attacked and burned by pirates.

Hawkins's galleons were lighter, faster, and more easily maneuvered, than the clumsy Spanish galleons. Instead of large numbers of soldiers, they carried two rows of small but powerful guns. They could shoot a cannonball over 2,500 feet with great accuracy. Spanish guns shot a heavier ball—but over only half the distance. English ships could hit Spanish ships while still out of range of the Spanish guns. Moreover, they could move quickly and fire their guns rapidly from different positions.

With these ships and methods Hawkins, Drake, and the English fleet defeated the Spanish Armada. Only 67 Spanish ships returned to Spain. Half were so badly damaged that they never sailed again. But the Spaniards learned an important lesson: sea power did not mean having the largest ships but the speediest, most maneuverable, and best-armed ones.

Life at Sea

Life at sea was always hard and dangerous. Below decks it was dark, smelly, airless and often very damp. Rats and cockroaches were common and the food was usually too hard to chew or full of weevils. Working on the masts was always dangerous.

It was not surprising that most people had to be forced ('pressed') into joining the navy to serve on galleons. Dreadful living conditions and lack of fresh food led to illness which, on a long voyage, caused more deaths than battle. In high winds seamen had to climb the tall masts and crawl along the rigging to haul in sails or fit new ones. Many fell to their deaths on the decks. Others might be badly injured by a mast that snapped in the wind. During calm weather the crew would be occupied in repairing sails, checking ropes, swabbing the decks and cleaning the guns. The captain, who lived much more comfortably in his own quarters and with special food, would spend his day plotting the course and writing his log. The officers saw to it that his orders were put into effect by the crew.

Battle at Sea

Control of the sea was important for all those countries which had overseas territories. Battles were fought between opposing galleons which attempted to sail alongside each other in order to fire a 'broadside' of cannon and inflict as much damage as possible on the enemy ship. Loss of life during sea battles was generally heavy.

Above: A galleon sets sail. Seamen hanging on the mainyard, unfurl the mainsail, while others in the main top adjust the rigging. The sails on the other two masts (the foremast and the mizzen) have already been unfurled.

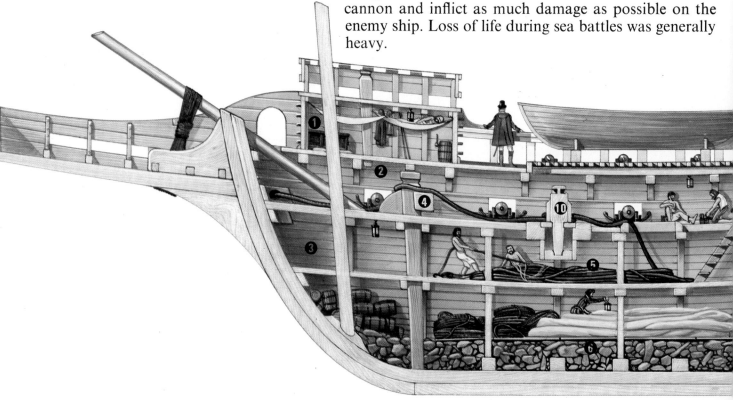

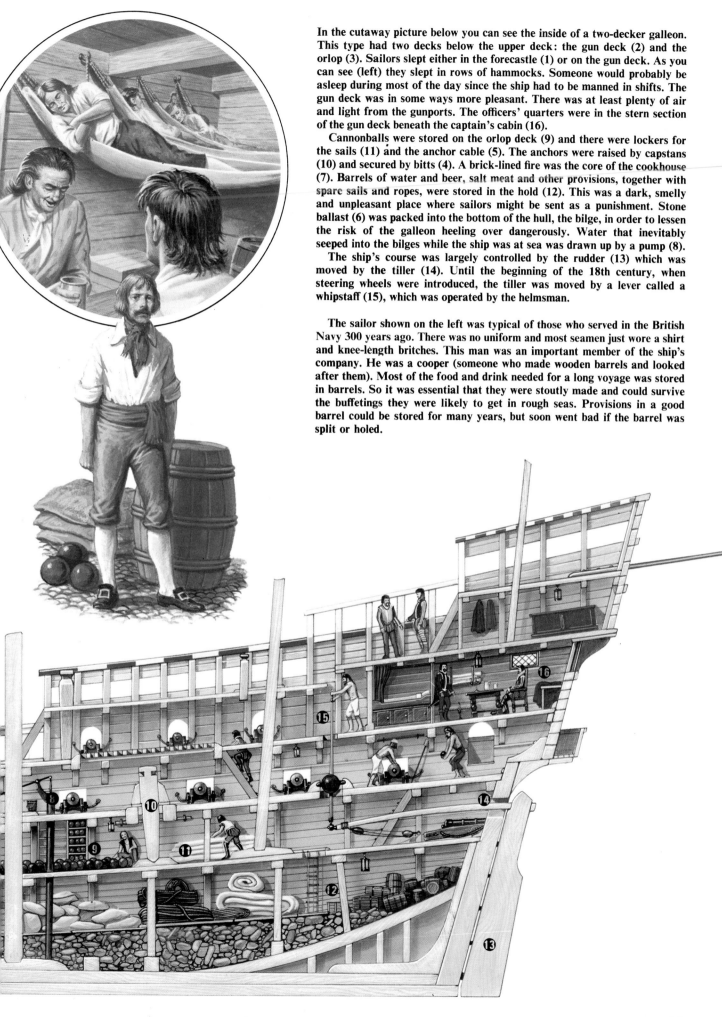

In the cutaway picture below you can see the inside of a two-decker galleon. This type had two decks below the upper deck: the gun deck (2) and the orlop (3). Sailors slept either in the forecastle (1) or on the gun deck. As you can see (left) they slept in rows of hammocks. Someone would probably be asleep during most of the day since the ship had to be manned in shifts. The gun deck was in some ways more pleasant. There was at least plenty of air and light from the gunports. The officers' quarters were in the stern section of the gun deck beneath the captain's cabin (16).

Cannonballs were stored on the orlop deck (9) and there were lockers for the sails (11) and the anchor cable (5). The anchors were raised by capstans (10) and secured by bitts (4). A brick-lined fire was the core of the cookhouse (7). Barrels of water and beer, salt meat and other provisions, together with spare sails and ropes, were stored in the hold (12). This was a dark, smelly and unpleasant place where sailors might be sent as a punishment. Stone ballast (6) was packed into the bottom of the hull, the bilge, in order to lessen the risk of the galleon heeling over dangerously. Water that inevitably seeped into the bilges while the ship was at sea was drawn up by a pump (8).

The ship's course was largely controlled by the rudder (13) which was moved by the tiller (14). Until the beginning of the 18th century, when steering wheels were introduced, the tiller was moved by a lever called a whipstaff (15), which was operated by the helmsman.

The sailor shown on the left was typical of those who served in the British Navy 300 years ago. There was no uniform and most seamen just wore a shirt and knee-length britches. This man was an important member of the ship's company. He was a cooper (someone who made wooden barrels and looked after them). Most of the food and drink needed for a long voyage was stored in barrels. So it was essential that they were stoutly made and could survive the buffetings they were likely to get in rough seas. Provisions in a good barrel could be stored for many years, but soon went bad if the barrel was split or holed.

The Age of Kings

In the 1600s kings were the most important people in Europe. They believed they had been appointed to rule by God himself.

When Louis XIV of France was a boy, he wrote: 'Homage is owed to kings. They do as they please.' Paying homage meant that everyone had to obey the king. Kings believed they had a 'divine right' to rule. They believed that a king had to answer only to God for his actions. So no one could tell a king what he should do.

Both Louis XIV of France and Charles I of England believed this. But their fortunes were very different.

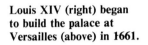

Louis XIV (right) began to build the palace at Versailles (above) in 1661.

Below: Hunting was Louis' favorite sport.

Above left: Louis had a council of state to advise him, but its ministers had no real power. Below: Life was often dull at Versailles, but there were parties, music, dancing and entertainers.

The Sun King

Louis XIV was one of the greatest kings of France. He made his country strong and increased its lands by war.

Louis became king when he was only 4 years old, in 1643. When he was 23 he took charge of the government. His 72-year rule was the longest in modern European history.

To make sure he had no rivals, Louis did not give government jobs to his relatives or to the nobles. Instead he chose humbler people as his ministers. His most famous and clever minister was Jean-Baptiste Colbert, the son of a draper. Such people were pleased to serve the King, and so gain wealth and high position.

Louis was also a great admirer of art and literature. He encouraged a number of artists and had many

In the English Civil War it was Oliver Cromwell and his New Model Army of plainly dressed Roundheads who finally beat the King's splendidly clad Cavaliers.

plays performed at his court. Louis himself danced the part of the Sun in a court ballet. This gave him the nickname 'the Sun King'.

The Court at Versailles
Louis built a splendid palace at Versailles, near Paris. He made his nobles live there instead of on their own estates. Louis wanted to keep an eye on them to make sure they did not plot against him. Life at Versailles was luxurious. The huge palace was filled with fine paintings and furniture. There were beautiful gardens with fountains and marble statues. The nobles whiled away their time with elaborate entertainments.

Charles I and Parliament
The reign of Charles I of England was very different from that of Louis XIV. Charles became king in 1625. He was a shy man, with a stammer, bow legs, and a stubborn nature. He hated to be opposed. But the members of the English Parliament were also very stubborn and just as determined to get their own way.

Parliament wanted to advise the King on how to govern the country. Its members wanted to decide what taxes he should raise and whom he should appoint as his ministers.

Charles refused. Instead he dismissed Parliament and ruled without it for 11 years, from 1629 to 1640. But without Parliament he could not raise money through taxes.

The English Civil War
In 1642 Parliament waged war against Charles. Led by Oliver Cromwell, the 'Roundhead' soldiers defeated the King's 'Cavaliers', and Charles was captured. Parliament accused the King of being a tyrant and a traitor. He was tried, found guilty, and executed in 1649. For Charles the 'divine right of Kings' had led only to disaster.

The New World

After the discovery of the New World, a fierce competition began among the countries of Europe to grab as much of it as possible.

For many years before Columbus crossed the Atlantic, the Aztecs of Mexico had believed in a prophecy: one day their white-skinned, bearded god Quetzalcoatl would return to them.

In 1519 Hernan Cortés led 550 Spanish *conquistadores* (conquerors) into Tenochtitlan, the Aztec capital. Cortés, white-skinned and bearded, appeared to the Aztecs to be their long-promised god. They met the Spaniards peacefully. But within two years, the Spaniards had conquered the Aztecs, killing many of them.

Montezuma, the Aztec ruler, was taken prisoner soon after the Spaniards arrived in Tenochtitlan. The Spaniards told Montezuma what orders to give his people. The Aztecs did not resist because they had been taught always to obey their ruler's commands.

The Puritans settled in America in 1620. They had left England to find a place where they could worship as they wished. These Pilgrim Fathers, as they are now called, established a colony at Plymouth, Massachusetts. Within 20 years the colony had a population of 20,000 people.

French
Spanish
English
Dutch

Left: The map shows how America had been divided up by 1650. Spain had the largest colonial empire in the New World. It was also the richest, and it made Spain the most powerful country in Europe for many years. In time Spain ruled all of South America except Brazil, a colony of the Portuguese, and the Guianas, settled by the British, Dutch, and French.

The Spanish Empire

A few years later Francisco Pizarro, another conquistador, conquered the Incas of Peru. He captured the Inca king, Atahualpa, and killed him after a roomful of gold had been collected as a ransom for his release. The Spaniards shipped all the gold to Spain. Spain soon had a huge empire in South and Central America, which it was to keep until the early 1800s.

Traders and Pilgrims

North America was settled in a very different way from South America. The first settlers were probably French fur traders, who traveled into the Canadian wilderness in search of animals such as the beaver, fox, wolf, and bear.

The first successful English settlement in the New World was at Jamestown, Virginia in 1607. More famous is the arrival of Puritans on the *Mayflower* at Plymouth, Massachusetts in 1620.

The British Colonies

Other English colonies were established along the eastern seaboard. In 1609 Henry Hudson sailed past what is now New York City into the river that bears his name. He claimed the region for the Dutch, who soon established a colony there. Its chief city, New Amsterdam, became New York when the English took over in 1664.

The French settlements, that had begun with the fur trade in Canada, soon spread south into the Ohio and Mississippi River valleys. As the English trappers and frontiersmen moved farther west, they clashed with the French. During the Seven Years' War in Europe (1756-1763) the English and French, each with different Indian tribes on their side, fought fiercely in North America. One of the great battles was at Quebec in Canada, when a British force under General Wolfe captured the city from the French, led by the Marquis de Montcalm. Both generals were killed in the battle. The French were finally forced to give up their territories, and Canada came under British rule like

After 1665 England and Spain fought over who owned Jamaica. Henry Morgan was a privateer in this war. He seized treasure from Spanish settlements and ships. He was knighted by King Charles II and made Deputy Governor of Jamaica, which England won by 1670.

its American neighbors, the 13 colonies to the south.

The rush of settlers to the New World soon caused a clash with the native Indian tribes, who saw their traditional hunting grounds being taken over. Many agreements about land were made with the Indians, but were often broken. Gradually, the Indians were pushed farther and farther west.

Below: Fort Garry was one of the Hudson's Bay Company's trading posts in Canada. The Company's agents traded cloth and beads with the Indians for furs, which brought high prices in England.

Charting the Pacific

Cook's voyages to Tahiti and to Australia produced a wealth of new scientific information.

In Botany Bay naturalists who were traveling with Cook picked 1,300 plants unknown to Europeans, and carefully sketched them.

In 1768 Captain James Cook set sail for the Pacific. People knew little about this vast ocean, which covers one third of the Earth. When Cook's last voyage ended in 1779, they knew far more.

James Cook was a Yorkshireman, born in 1728. At 18 he was apprenticed to a merchant shipowner. In 1755 he volunteered for the Royal Navy. He earned rapid promotion and in 1768 the Admiralty placed him in command of H.M.S. *Endeavour Bark*, to carry out a voyage of scientific and geographical discovery in the vast, uncharted Pacific Ocean.

Cook's Voyages of Discovery

Cook sailed from Plymouth, England on August 25, 1768. Eight months later he landed on the Pacific island of Tahiti. Cook was not the first European to explore the area. Spanish, French, and Dutch sailors had been there before. But they had discovered little about the Pacific and its lands.

Cook, however, was a great navigator and mapmaker. He had learned to make very accurate maps and took care to make detailed notes on all he saw on his travels. During his three long voyages, between 1768 and 1779, he crossed and recrossed the ocean. He sailed from the frozen waters of the Arctic to the pack ice and icebergs of the Antarctic.

Exploring New Zealand and Australia

Cook sailed round New Zealand, which had been discovered by the Dutch. He made an accurate map of its coastline. Then he sailed westwards towards the east coast of Australia. Earlier explorers had visited other parts of Australia before without realizing how large the new continent was. They found the land dry and rocky, but on the east coast it was green and fertile.

The map shows the route Cook took on his first voyage to the Pacific.

In New Zealand Cook met the warlike Maoris, who paddled great war canoes and tattooed their faces. They were also skilled craftsmen. On the right are some examples of Maori art, carved from wood, whalebone and jade.

The Landing in Botany Bay

The naturalists and artists who travelled with Cook found many trees, flowers, and animals to study. There were so many new and unusual plants growing in one bay that Cook called it Botany Bay. On August 23, 1770 he took possession of the country for Britain.

Cook also visited many small islands in the Pacific. He was fascinated by the islanders' religious ceremonies and dances, and enjoyed feasting with the chieftains. The people were so friendly that Cook called the Tonga group of islands the 'Friendly Islands'. But not all the Pacific Islanders were friendly. In 1779 Cook was murdered in Hawaii during a quarrel with some Hawaiians. He left behind him a wealth of information, charts, and maps, and paved the way for the settlement of Australia and New Zealand.

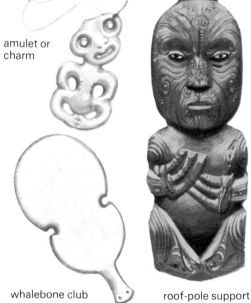

amulet or charm

whalebone club

roof-pole support

Below: Off the east coast of Australia, Cook's ship struck the Great Barrier Reef. Aborigines watched with interest as the crew repaired the damage.

The Revolution in Agriculture

Farming methods changed very little for centuries. Then during the 1700s they gradually began to be changed.

We call this period of change the Agricultural Revolution.

There are many reasons why farming methods began to change. The most important cause was the steady rise in population. With improvements in medicine and hygiene, people lived longer. As more factories were built, towns grew bigger. In order to provide food for all these people, farming had to be improved.

The most important change was the enclosure of fields. In the Middle Ages most villages had been surrounded by three large open fields. Every villager owned a number of strips of land in each field. He could also probably graze his sheep and cattle on common land.

This system caused many problems. Firstly, it was difficult to drain the land properly. Secondly, if a farmer did not look after his land weeds spread to his neighbors'. Thirdly, a farmer might have to walk a long way from one strip to his next one. The answer was to split the land so that each man had one small field surrounded by a hedge.

There was a three-year rotation of crops. Each field would be left unsown (fallow) every third year. This allowed the soil to recover its goodness. A British farmer nicknamed 'Turnip' Townshend introduced a four-year rotation on his farm. He grew clover and turnips in rotation with wheat and barley. No field was left fallow

for these crops. This improved the soil as well as giving more food, including winter food for the animals.

Another Englishman, Robert Bakewell, had as his main concern the improvement of the quality of his cattle and sheep. He used root crops as winter feed. He bred from the best animals to develop fatter cattle and sheep. Other farmers took up his ideas.

New Machines on the Land

Until the 1700s most people lived in the country. Many of them worked on the land and grew just enough food for themselves. In those days there was very little machinery to help the farmers. Each village probably owned one plow with a plowshare made by the local blacksmith. Mules and oxen would draw the plow up and down the farmers' strips of land. Then seed would be scattered in the furrows. They harvested the crops with scythes and sickles.

Farming in this way was very wasteful of time and effort, and produced poor quality crops.

Left: The domestication of animals greatly increased people's ability to farm the land. Animals, like the ox and the donkey (far left), could turn a water-lifting machine. Oxen and horses (left) could pull a plow. But for centuries simple agricultural machinery was developed very little.

Below: In 1831 Cyrus McCormick unveiled his reaping machine to the world. It was ten years before it began to be generally used.

As farming entered the 18th century, however, it was to undergo radical changes. In 1701 an Englishman named Jethro Tull invented a seed drill that eliminated the hand sowing of seeds and, a few years later, a horse-drawn hoe that both cultivated and weeded. By the end of the century Eli Whitney had revolutionized the cotton industry in the United States. His cotton gin simplified the separation of the seed from the cotton plant. And in 1834 Cyrus McCormick patented the first harvesting machine—the reaper. This machine made quick work of cutting grain, thereby replacing the hand scythe.

Other inventions developed during the 19th century include the thresher, made by John and Hiram Pitts, and the steel plow, by an Illinois farmer named John Deere. Scientists also began combining chemicals for insecticides and fertilizers that would make plants healthier and easier to grow.

The Effects of the Argicultural Revolution

Although machinery brought about great improvements in agriculture, new inventions were not always welcomed by farm workers at that time. New, more efficient machines meant that fewer workers were needed. Fearing unemployment, many farm workers and their families moved from the country to the towns to work in and around the new factories. Ironically, the improved farming methods that prompted them to move into the towns enabled the farmers to feed the growing number of townspeople with less labor.

Right: The modern pig is a very different animal to the wild boar from which it has been developed. For centuries the domestic pig changed little from its wild ancestors. Then, following the ideas of Robert Bakewell, the pioneer animal breeder, farmers began to concern themselves with improved breeding methods. They kept the animals best suited to their needs and used them to breed the next generation. They tried to breed animals that fattened quickly and could resist disease.

89

The Age of Revolution

The late 1700s were the beginning of an age of revolution. In America and France the people over-turned their old systems of government.

The American Colonies

One night in 1773 a group of American colonists, disguised as Indians, boarded three ships in Boston harbor and emptied their cargoes of tea into the water. This raid was a protest against a tax on tea levied by British parliament—a tax the colonists considered unfair. Their slogan, 'No taxation without representation,' meant that they wanted to have a say in making laws that affected them.

The War of Independence

On April 19, 1775, British forces marched into Lexington, Massachusetts. They were on their way to destroy military supplies stored by colonists at nearby Concord. At Lexington the British met unexpected resistance from 70 armed 'minutement' (so named because the American soldiers could prepare for battle in a minute). A shot was fired—'the shot heard round the world'—and the battle begins.

Within days nearly 16,000 colonists had taken up arms. General George Washington, later the first president of the United States, led the American patriots in war against the British.

At first the war went badly for the Americans. But in July 1776 they united their efforts in the creation and signing of the Declaration of Independence, and after a series of American victories in 1777, France came to the aid of the colonists.

In 1781 General Cornwallis, the British commander, was forced to surrender. In 1783, in the Treaty of Paris, the British agreed to the independence of the 13 colonies as the United States of America.

Above: The 'Boston Tea Party' so angered the British that they closed the port of Boston until the tea was paid for. This made the colonists more determined to end British rule in America.

Left: Backed up by the French, the American army compelled the British forces to surrender at Yorktown, Virginia in October 1781. The peace treaty was signed in 1783.

In 1789 the people of Paris attacked the Bastille, a prison, in an attempt to capture weapons and free political prisoners. The fall of the Bastille marked the beginning of the French Revolution.

Discontent in France

While the Americans were gaining their independence, discontent was growing in France.

The French felt that they were ruled unfairly. The King, Louis XVI, did not seem to care that many people were poor and hungry, and heavily taxed. The middle classes, or *bourgeoisie*, such as merchants and lawyers, were also heavily taxed, but had little say in the government. Even the nobles and rich churchmen, who paid no taxes, were angry because the King would not let them share in ruling France.

Down with the King!

By 1789 the three social classes, or 'Estates', opposed the King: the Church (First Estate), the nobles (Second Estate), and the workers and *bourgeoisie* (Third Estate). The French States General (parliament), made up of the three Estates, was called for the first time in 164 years.

On July 14, 1789, fighting broke out in Paris. Soon the rebellion against the King spread throughout France.

The Reign of Terror

Before long the unity of the Three Estates broke up. The Third Estate seized power and took revenge on its old enemies, the Church and nobles. A 'reign of terror' began.

In 1793 King Louis and his Queen, Marie Antoinette, were put to death by the guillotine, a machine that chopped off their heads. Hundreds of priests and nobles were executed. The leaders of the Revolution, Danton, Marat, and Robespierre, ruled with great violence. In the end they too met their deaths.

What Did the Revolution Achieve?

By 1804 France had an emperor, Napoleon. But the ideas of the French Revolution lived on. The new American republic, too, inspired people everywhere. Over the next 50 years the spirit of independence spread to many countries in Europe and to the Spanish colonies in South America.

Hundreds of nobles were guillotined in the 'Reign of Terror'. The leaders of the Revolution put to death anyone who did not agree with them.

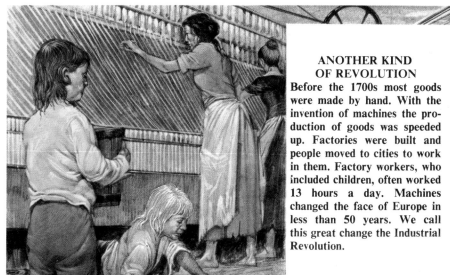

ANOTHER KIND OF REVOLUTION

Before the 1700s most goods were made by hand. With the invention of machines the production of goods was speeded up. Factories were built and people moved to cities to work in them. Factory workers, who included children, often worked 13 hours a day. Machines changed the face of Europe in less than 50 years. We call this great change the Industrial Revolution.

The Spirit of Freedom

The success of the American and French revolutions had a great effect on the rest of the world. In Europe and in the Spanish colonies of southern America, people saw the chance of gaining their freedom.

Revolt in Haiti

In 1791, as the French struggled to overthrow their king, one of their own colonies seized the chance to free itself from French rule. The slaves on the Caribbean island of Haiti rebelled against their French masters. After a bloody uprising, Toussaint L'Ouverture, a former slave, took control. Later, when Napoleon came to power in France, he sent a French army to recapture Haiti. Toussaint was sent to prison in France. But the French troops in Haiti fell victim to yellow fever. Badly weakened, the army was finally defeated by the Haitians in 1803. In 1804, Haiti declared its independence from France.

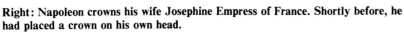

■ French Empire
□ Areas controlled by Napoleon
■ Countries friendly to Napoleon

Right: Napoleon crowns his wife Josephine Empress of France. Shortly before, he had placed a crown on his own head.

Below: Napoleon made a terrible mistake in attacking Russia in 1812. He was forced to retreat through the snows of the Russian winter.

'The Liberator'

In 1805, a 22-year-old Venezuelan, Simon Bolivar, took a solemn vow to free his country from Spanish rule.

Most of South America was part of a huge Spanish empire over 300 years old. The colonies were strictly ruled by Spanish governors and officials. Bolivar knew that he could not defeat the Spanish troops in open battle. But he realized that his men knew the countryside much better than the Spaniards. They could take short cuts across country; the Spaniards had to keep to the roads.

Between 1811 and 1825, Bolivar and his followers fought a long, difficult war against the Spaniards. In time his armies freed the whole of northern South America from Spanish rule. Six new republics were born: Venezuela, Colombia, Ecuador, Peru, Bolivia, and Panama. Bolivar—'The Liberator'—had kept his vow.

Revolutions in Europe

In Europe, Napoleon Bonaparte led the armies of revolutionary France to great victories after 1796. In 1804 he crowned himself Emperor of France and ruler of the huge European empire he had conquered. But in 1815, Napoleon was defeated at Waterloo by the British and Prussians. He died in exile on the lonely South Atlantic island of St. Helena in 1821.

After Napoleon's death, the empire crumbled and France was once again governed by kings. It was almost as if the French revolution of 1789 had never happened. But the ideas that had started the French and American revolutions still simmered. In 1830 and again in 1848, these ideas again drove the French to rebel against their king.

Between 1848 and 1867, the great Italian patriot-soldier, Giuseppe Garibaldi, fought against the Austrians and Spaniards to make Italy a united and independent country. In 1860 his 'redshirts', only 1,000 strong, captured Sicily and the area south of Naples.

The South American wars of independence were fought with great savagery on both sides.

Other peoples copied the French example: the Poles, Belgians, and Italians rose in 1830; the Austrians, Hungarians, Italians and Slavs in 1848. These revolutions were all separate, but took place for very similar reasons. Bad harvests had caused famine. Many people were homeless and out of work. Revolution seemed the only way to change things. The rulers who resisted the revolutions of 1848 finally restored order. But the revolutionaries had not failed completely. After 1848, no European ruler could ignore the voice of the people.

Steam Engines and Factories

What is known as the Industrial Revolution was brought about by the discovery that machines could be made to provide power. The development of steam power led to very rapid changes, but that very speed caused a great deal of hardship and misery.

A series of inventions and technical innovations in the second half of the 18th century greatly increased the output of manufactured goods in Britain. They included new spinning machines and looms, the coke-smelting process and the introduction of crucible cast steel. But of greatest importance was the steam engine, which made possible the replacement of small workshops by large factories.

The Steam Engines

The first practical steam engine was invented in 1698 by Thomas Savery. It was used to pump water out of mines. It consisted of a heated boiler from which steam passed to a cylinder. This was connected to the mine-water and, when the cylinder was cooled, the steam condensed and created a vacuum which sucked up the water.

Improvements were later made by Thomas Newcomen whose machines proved very reliable. But they were not very efficient since heat was wasted when the cylinder was constantly cooled. James Watt built a separate condenser to overcome the problem. Then, in 1782, he linked the piston in the cylinder by using the sun-and-planet gear to provide a revolving motion. This turned a shaft which itself was capable of driving machinery.

The Social Effects of the Industrial Revolution

Large machines led to large factories. Towns grew up around these factories. Drab lines of houses were built for the factory workers. Work in the factories was hard and long, and the wages were kept low so that profits would rise. At home life was often squalid and miserable because people had barely enough money to pay for their food and clothing. In Europe, times were particularly bad after the Napoleonic Wars when trade declined and prices rose.

Matters did not improve a great deal throughout the rest of the 19th century. Children often worked long hours because parents needed the money they brought in and employers needed their labor. In the cities an almost total neglect of public health led to the unchecked spread of disease and death at an early age. Three or four families often occupied a single, poorly-lit house with no running water.

Novelist Charles Dickens did much to expose the evils of child labor and other social ills in his books, such as *Oliver Twist*. Gradually, due to social reformers' efforts to increase public awareness, laws were passed to protect the young and the needy. In 1886 skilled laborers in the U.S. formed the American Federation of Labor. Under the leadership of Samuel Gompers, this union found the strength to bargain with powerful industrialists for better wages and working conditions. Thus, a way was born to control exploitation of the worker. Of course, the reformers and unions did not cure these social ills, but they gave people hope for a better life.

The textile industry was one of the first to feel the effects of the Industrial Revolution. Huge mills were built next to rivers. Steam engines, linked with power looms on the mill floor by a system of belts and pulleys, provided the power. Women and children often worked at the looms because it was not considered to be strenuous work. In fact it was extremely tiring and could be dangerous as well. Sixteen hours a day in the factories was not uncommon. The workers had to stand at their machines all this time with only very short breaks. The light was bad and the air soon got stale. Accidents were common since the machines had no safety guards. And, at the end of the week, wages were very low.

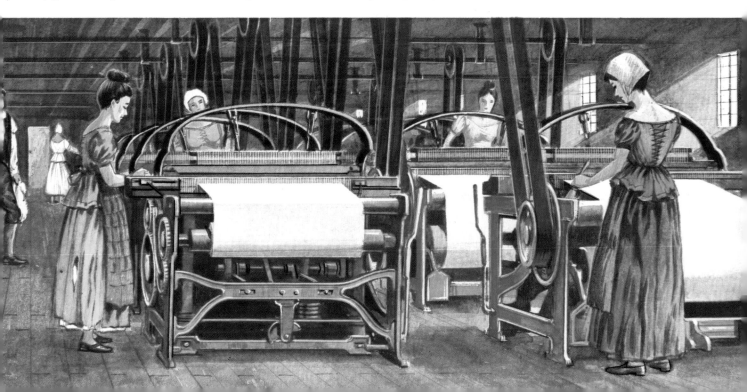

The first journey by rail was a grand occasion. A man went ahead of the engine with a red flag to warn people.

Steam and Science

The Transport Age

With the arrival of the Industrial Revolution, goods had to be carried faster and farther than before. Coal and other heavy raw materials had to be moved to supply the factories. Manufactured goods had to be taken to the ports and towns.

But in the 1700s transport was difficult. Roads were very bad. They were muddy, stony and full of holes. Horse-drawn carts and coaches were slow. It was not always possible to travel far by river. Often low bridges blocked the way.

Sometimes land-owners refused to let boats pass along their part of the river.

The Canal Builders

In 1760 the engineer James Brindley started to build the Bridgewater Canal in England. It ran from the Duke of Bridgewater's coal mines to his mills in Manchester. Before long canals were being built all over England. Canal boats traveled from the factories to the ports, or to the towns where the goods were sold. By 1830 Britain had more than 4,000 miles of canals.

This railway bridge near Birmingham, England, was built by Thomas Telford. It crosses a canal and, here, a horse is on the towpath pulling a boat along the canal. The laborers who built the canals were known as 'navigators', or 'navvies' for short. It was a rough, hard-working life, but their exertions changed much of the face of Britain.

On November 21, 1783, a hot air balloon built by two Frenchmen, Joseph and Jacques Montgolfier, flew nearly five miles in 25 minutes This was the first step in the conquest of the air.

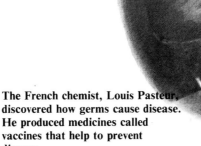

The French chemist, Louis Pasteur, discovered how germs cause disease. He produced medicines called vaccines that help to prevent disease.

The Coming of the Railways

In the early 1800s engineers discovered how to use the steam engine to make a 'locomotive' move on iron rails.

On September 27, 1825, a large and excited crowd saw the steam locomotive, *Locomotion*, built by George Stephenson, pull 12 coal wagons and 21 passenger wagons containing 450 brave people along the new railway between Stockton and Darlington in northern England. This was the world's first passenger railway.

At first people thought that railways were dangerous, and that people would die if they went over 30 miles an hour.

The Wonder of Steam

Soon people were building railways everywhere. Everywhere people were excited by the new discovery of steam power. An adaptation of the steam engine was soon appearing on waterways in the United States and Europe—the steamboat. Robert Fulton's steam-powered riverboat, the *Clermont*, made its first voyage in 1807, when it steamed the 150 miles from New York City to Albany. The first trans-Atlantic voyage by a steamboat was made by the American *Savannah* in 1819. Actually, the *Savannah* was a fully rigged sailing ship equipped with steam-powered side-wheels.

Science and Medicine

It was not only in transport that scientific knowledge was having an impact. A series of new discoveries were made about disease. Florence Nightingale proved that good nursing and cleaner hospitals helped to prevent infection and death. The French chemist, Louis Pasteur, discovered how germs caused disease. He produced medicines called vaccines to prevent some diseases.

Many people began to think that science and inventions would solve all the world's problems.

Below: The Eiffel Tower was built for a great exhibition in Paris in 1889. This exhibition displayed the latest new machinery and inventions. Thousands of people went to see this new world.

The Egyptians joined the two ends of their boats with a thick rope. This stopped it from breaking in two over a wave.

The Greeks and Romans built war galleys and merchant ships. They used the power of both oarsmen and the wind.

This sailing ship had a tall poop at the stern to stop the ship being swamped.

The Story of Ships

The story of ships began when a prehistoric man first used a floating log to help him across a river. Today, sleek ocean liners cross the Atlantic in under four days.

The oldest pictures of boats are carved or drawn on pottery and stone in the lands of the Middle East, where the Sumerian and Egyptian civilizations flourished, and in the Indus valley of Pakistan. They show that these ancient people built boats from bundles of reeds bound together with ropes. Later, wooden planks were used to build bigger and stronger boats called galleys. They were rowed with oars or driven by sails.

The Greek and Roman warships were large, fast galleys with an iron ram at the front. They were rowed by two or three banks of oarsmen who were usually slaves.

In the Middle Ages, sails replaced oars as the normal means of propelling a ship. Small, sturdy sailing ships brought goods from distant lands. Sea battles were fought between tall, powerful galleons.

For hundreds of years heavily armed galleons fought sea battles. Some carried more than a hundred guns. The gunners aimed for the waterline of an enemy ship so that the sea would rush in. They also aimed at the mast, for, if the sails were brought down, the ship would be helpless.

M. TRIM. 76

The clippers were the fastest sailing ships. They had a sharp prow to cut through the waves.

The earliest steamships still carried sails. They were driven by paddlewheels. Today's ships are driven by propellers.

The Coming of Steam Power

When the steam engine was invented, ships no longer had to rely on wind. The steam engines could move larger, heavier vessels, better than sails. Huge ships, built of iron, gradually replaced the wooden sailing ships.

The last of the great sailing ships were the graceful clippers which carried tea from China and wool from Australia. They were designed for speed and carried four and even five tall masts of billowing sails. It was many years before steamships could go as fast as a clipper in a good wind.

At night ships carry white lights on the fore and main masts. On the port (left hand) they have a red light. On the starboard (right hand) they carry a green light. From the pattern of lights, sailors can tell in which direction a ship is sailing.

Trains and Railways

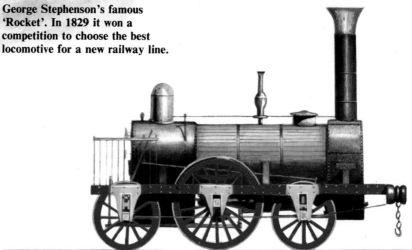

George Stephenson's famous 'Rocket'. In 1829 it won a competition to choose the best locomotive for a new railway line.

Below: Robert Stephenson's 'Patentee' locomotive which ran on the Liverpool and Manchester Railway in 1834.

Travel by road was slow and uncomfortable 200 years ago. Then came the railways.

In the early 1800s railways grew rapidly throughout the eastern United States, but none extended across the Mississippi River and into the undeveloped regions of the West. In 1862 Congress passed the Pacific Railroad Act that chartered the Union Pacific and Central Pacific railroads to begin laying rail for the first transcontinental railway.

Both companies employed thousands of unskilled laborers—mostly Civil War veterans, and European and Chinese immigrants. In 1863 the Central Pacific began to lay track east from Sacramento, California. Two years later, from a point near Omaha, Nebraska, the Union Pacific started laying track west. On May 10, 1869, officials from the two companies met at a point in Utah to drive in the last spike, marking the completion of their monumental task. This achievement was to change the face of North America through improved freight and passenger transport.

In 1936 a streamlined British locomotive, the 'Mallard', reached a speed of 125 miles per hour. This record has never been bettered by a steam locomotive.

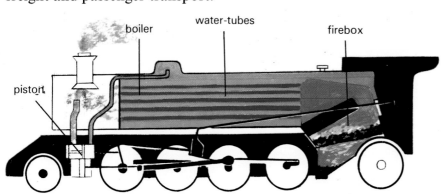

In a steam locomotive coal is burned in the firebox. Water running through tubes in the boiler is heated by the burning fuel and turns to steam. Steam takes up much more space than water and the pressure in the boiler increases. Steam is allowed to escape from the boiler by moving a piston in a cylinder. The piston in turn moves the driving rod, which turns the wheels of the locomotive.

Huge diesel locomotives haul freight cars on the long journey across America.

Until the beginning of this century the railways had no rivals. Then the motor car and airplane were invented. Railways were used less and some lines closed. Now, new trains can travel faster than cars. And there are hovertrains, which glide on a cushion of air. The French Aerotrain, for example, is a hovertrain, which has already traveled at over 200 miles per hour.

With these advances many railways are becoming faster and more comfortable than ever before.

Within 25 years of the first railway, almost every country in Europe had built one. Enough track had been laid to stretch around the world. Soon people could travel across Europe, Asia, and North America by rail.

Steam locomotives grew bigger and more powerful. For over a century they hauled passenger trains and freight cars all over the world. But there are few left now. They were replaced by diesel and electric locomotives, which are cleaner, quieter, and cheaper to run.

Diesel locomotives have oil-burning engines like those in large trucks. Electric locomotives are driven by electric motors. They get electricity from overhead wires or from a third, 'live', rail.

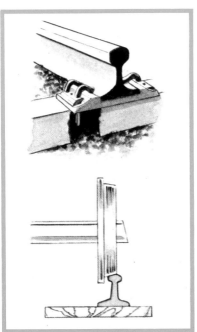

The wheels of locomotives and carriages are specially shaped to run on the curved surface of a rail. A flange on the inside of each wheel makes sure that it cannot leave the rail. Railway tracks are set at a fixed width.

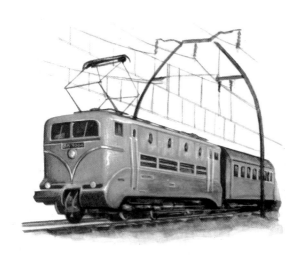

Electric locomotives have traveled at 200 miles per hour on straight stretches of track. They are clean and quiet. This type picks up its electric current from overhead power lines.

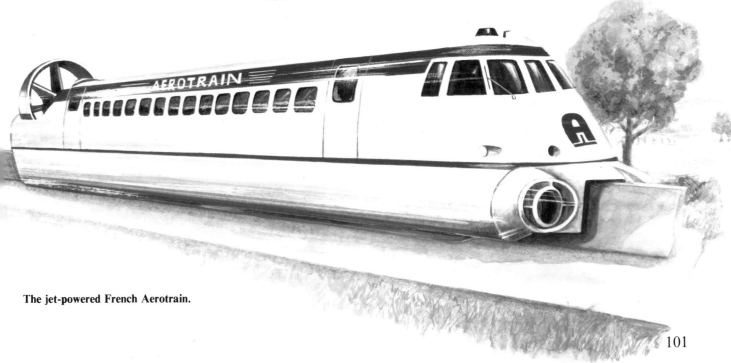

The jet-powered French Aerotrain.

101

Winning the West

During the 1800s thousands of men, women, and children set out across America on a long, perilous journey. They went to settle the huge, rich, but wild lands of the American West, the little-known country beyond the Appalachian Mountains.

The first 'pioneers' traveled on foot, on horseback, or in wagons. It was said that a pioneer needed just two things to survive: a gun to hunt food and fight off hostile Indians, and an axe to clear the forest land, make fences round his crops, and build a log cabin to live in.

The settlers also needed courage to face the hardships of the journey. There were high mountains and fast-flowing rivers to cross. They faced day after day of rolling prairie, where dust storms choked and blinded them and blizzards froze them.

The Promised Land
Why did people brave such dangers? Some went in search of adventure. Others went to make a new life. Many hoped to get rich. A frantic 'gold rush' began when gold was discovered in California in 1848. The Mormons went west to find a place where they could practice their religion in freedom.

Brigham Young

Daniel Boone

Davy Crockett

BLAZING THE TRAIL
The settlers followed the trails explored by frontiersmen. Often these men were hunters and trappers, such as Davy Crockett and Daniel Boone. Between 1804 and 1806 the explorers Meriwether Lewis and William Clark (top) mapped the Missouri River valley. Brigham Young was another pioneer. He led the Mormons to the Great Salt Lake in Utah in 1847.

Wonderful stories were told about the West and its riches. To many poor people in Europe, America sounded like the Promised Land.

Life on the Frontier

The settlers had to be tough, and lucky, to survive. Many died on the trail. If they survived and found a place to settle, life was still difficult and dangerous. Indian tribes were hostile because the settlers had invaded their lands, destroying forests and plowing fields where the Indians had been hunting and living for hundreds of years.

From the Old World to the New

After about 1840 thousands of immigrants came to America from Europe. They left behind lives of poverty and hardship. They crossed the Atlantic hoping to find better lives.

Most of the immigrants arrived with few possessions. They knew little about the land that was to be their home. Some settled in the East, but many more headed west.

Within days of their arrival in America, immigrants were traveling westward with the wagon trains. Some took the steamboats along the Mississippi River, and settled along the river banks. Later others traveled on the railways that were being built across the country.

From Coast to Coast

The original 13 states of the United States lay between the Appalachian Mountains and the Atlantic. But the boundary, or frontier, moved further west with each wave of settlers. Between about 1815, when the pioneers began settling the new lands, and 1890, when the western frontier of the United States was the Pacific Ocean, more than 3,000 miles away, the West was won.

Red Cloud

Geronimo

Sitting Bull

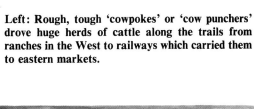

Left: Rough, tough 'cowpokes' or 'cow punchers' drove huge herds of cattle along the trails from ranches in the West to railways which carried them to eastern markets.

Left: As the wagon trains moved west, they crossed the lands of the Indians. Led by chiefs such as Red Cloud, Sitting Bull and Geronimo (top), some Indian tribes fought against the newcomers. But by 1890 all the tribes had been conquered and settled in special areas called reservations. The U.S. cavalry (above) protected the settlers against Indians and helped to keep peace in the West.

103

The Civil War

In the mid-1800s the United States suffered through a bloody civil war that ripped the country apart but ultimately bonded the states together as one nation like no other event in U.S. history.

At the time the American West was being settled the eastern states were developing as well but in very different ways. As the northern states became more industrialized they soon controlled most of the financial wealth of the nation. The strength of the southern states, however, lay in agriculture. From the time of the first settlements the southern economy was based on cotton and tobacco, crops that were dependent on slave labor. It was the moral issue of slavery that finally brought to a head the conflict between North and South.

For several hundred years Africans had been shipped across the Atlantic Ocean to be sold as slaves in America. There they worked on cotton, tobacco, and sugar plantations. Not until New Year's Day, 1863 were slaves in the United States set free by President Lincoln in the Emancipation Proclamation. In the midst of war, however, the South was in such turmoil that many former slaves remained on the plantations for a time.

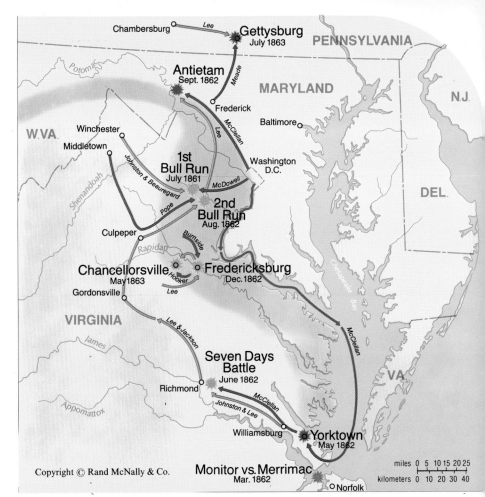

Copyright © Rand McNally & Co.

In the major battles during the first years of the war the Confederate offensive in the East was successful. But when General Lee invaded Yankee territory, once at Antietam, Maryland and again at Gettysburg, Pennsylvania, the Confederate armies had to retreat.

As northerners began protesting the continued existence of slavery in the United States, tension mounted until, by 1860, the nation was, in Abraham Lincoln's words, 'a house divided.' Abolitionists—people whose primary goal was to end slavery—prompted northerners to help slaves slip across borders into free states by way of a network called the *underground railroad*. As more and more slaves escaped to freedom, southern leaders called for federal legislation forcing the return of slaves to their owners.

The South Secedes
Passage of the Kansas-Nebraska Act in 1854 sparked heated debates between North and South. This legislation gave two new territories the responsibility of deciding for themselves whether to legalize or to outlaw slavery within their borders. Fighting, often armed and deadly, broke out among the dissident settlers.

As anti-slavery sentiment grew and northern politicians continued to press for federal legislation on economic issues, southern leaders determined that the South's best interests were not being taken into consideration by the nation as a whole. In December 1860, just after Abraham Lincoln was elected President, South Carolina became the first state to secede from the United States. Shortly after, seven more southern states also withdrew, and together they elected Jefferson Davis President of the Confederate States of America.

The War Between the States
In his inaugural address President Lincoln stated that secession was illegal but avoided mention of taking military action against the

Left: General George Pickett's charge up Cemetery Ridge at Gettysberg, Pennsylvania has often been referred to as 'the high water mark of the Confederacy.' Though loss of life in the Battle of Gettysburg was heavier for the North, the strength of the Confederate Army was hardest hit. General Lee would never again be able to undertake a major offensive against the North.

secessionist states. One month later Confederate soldiers captured Fort Sumter in the harbor of Charleston, South Carolina. When President Lincoln sent reinforcements the South interpreted his act as a declaration of war, and Virginia, North Carolina, Arkansas, and Tennessee joined the Confederacy.

Despite having fewer resources than the North, the Confederate armies won many decisive victories under the experienced leadership of General Robert E. Lee. Unfortunately, what both sides hoped would be a brief conflict turned into a full-scale civil war in which more Americans lost their lives than in any other war in history. Deaths, including those from disease, which was rampant in the overcrowded prison camps, totalled 529,332. The South suffered the worst damage since most of the battles took place on southern territory.

The war dragged on for four years until the commander of the Union armies, General Ulysses S. Grant, made his final march through Virginia. At the same time, General William T. Sherman and his troops burned a path across Georgia and the Carolinas, destroying anything that might help the South continue the war. On April 8, 1865, the generals of the Confederate and Union armies met at Appomattox Court House in Virginia where General Lee, knowing that a southern victory was hopeless, surrendered.

Developed during the American Civil War, the Gatling gun was the first successful machine gun.

At the end of the war, President Abraham Lincoln voiced his hopes for a quick reconstruction and reconciliation between North and South. The wisdom and foresight Lincoln had shown during the war carried over into his plans for the nation's recovery. But he would never see his plans fulfilled.

Six days after Lee's surrender to Grant, President Lincoln was fatally wounded by a gunshot while watching a play at the Ford Theater in Washington D.C. It was left to his successor, Andrew Johnson, to begin the slow restoration of the South and the reuniting of the nation.

Overseas Empires

From the middle of the eighteenth century European countries began to realize the importance of overseas possessions. Cheap labor (which, in the beginning, was usually slaves) could provide cheap raw materials much valued at home. Overseas posts could also be strategically important in times of war.

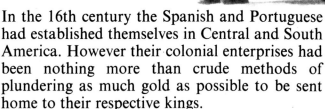

Originally the British had no intention of governing India. The East India Company merely wished to make money there, but occasionally the army had to intervene to protect British interests and commerce. Here, Britain's control of the seas gave her an immense advantage over her chief rival, France, since reinforcements could be quickly dispatched. In 1757 the Indian princes rebelled against the British, but troops under the command of Robert Clive defeated them at the Battle of Plassey. This victory gave the British control of the rich province of Bengal and marked the foundation of the British Empire in India.

In the 16th century the Spanish and Portuguese had established themselves in Central and South America. However their colonial enterprises had been nothing more than crude methods of plundering as much gold as possible to be sent home to their respective kings.

By the 18th century empire builders were more sophisticated and less cruel, but their main motive was still commercial. The British, who ended up with the largest overseas empire, initially had no wish to administer these lands. Indeed, it was trading companies in India and Canada which began the work of colonization. They involved the government when they had to ward off revolts by the local people or attacks by rivals.

The United States and Canada

In America, the British lost their most valuable territories almost before they had begun to establish their Empire. An attempt to force laws and taxes on a population that was not represented in the British Parliament led to the War of American Independence. The British were defeated by the American army and had to surrender their claims to this part of North America, which then became the United States of America.

In Canada, however, the British imposed their empire on the French in the east when General Wolfe defeated their forces at Quebec in 1759. In the north and west the Hudson's Bay Company set up numerous trading posts as they scoured the country for furs. These posts later became centers for administration. But the British Government had learned from its mistakes with the United States, and, during the 1840s and 50s, granted independence to the Canadian provinces, though they still remained loyal to the Crown.

Australia and New Zealand

Cook's voyage to the fertile and attractive eastern coast of Australia in 1770 signaled the beginning of British rule in that continent. Eighteen years later a batch of convicts was landed at Botany Bay and for many years the country was used as a dumping ground for undesirables. Gold and land attracted thousands of immigrants in the mid 19th century, and by the 1870s these people were allowed a considerable degree of self-government. In New Zealand, where good farming land attracted immigrants, the road to independence was much the same.

India: The Jewel in the Crown
By the start of the 19th century the British effectively ruled in India, although large tracts of land were theoretically the private domains of Indian princes. British rule was, to a large extent, enforced by Indian soldiers, called *Sepoys,* who were reliable and efficient. Insensitive treatment by the British authorities led, however, to a mutiny by these sepoys in 1857. Small British garrisons were surrounded by the mutineers at Cawnpore, Delhi and Lucknow, and when the Indians broke through the defenses they spared no one. British reinforcements eventually put down the rebellion and exacted a gruesome revenge. Because of its importance India remained part of the Empire until 1947.

The Scramble for Africa
In 1815 Britain bought Cape Colony in South Africa so that she could have a staging-post for ships going to India. Famous explorers like Livingstone and Speke opened up much of Eastern and Central Africa in the middle of the century. Then, in 1875, Disraeli, the British Prime Minister, bought a controlling interest in the newly opened Suez Canal through which ships could pass instead of going all the way around the Cape.

Other European countries had already begun to see the advantages of colonies in the continent; now they became jealous of Britain's ever-increasing territorial strength. The French seized much of West Africa, though the British had already established themselves in the vast country of Nigeria. The King of the Belgians claimed and settled a vast territory in Central Africa called the Belgian Congo. Germany, Italy, Spain and Portugal also snatched territories.

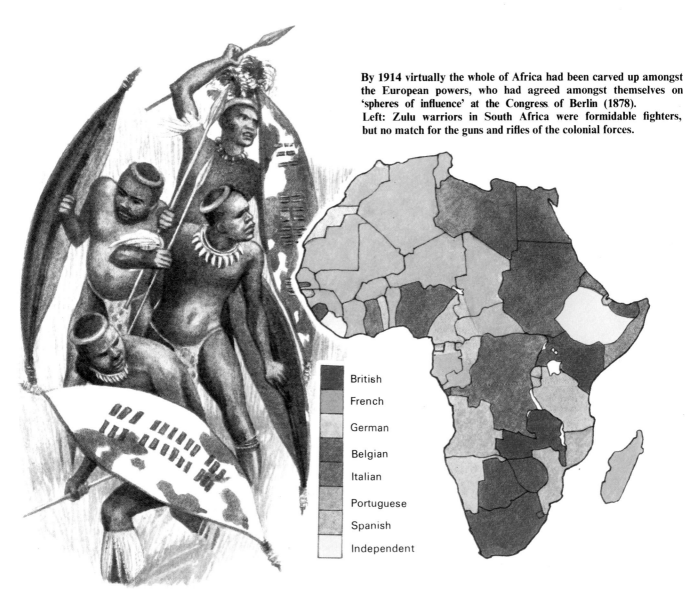

By 1914 virtually the whole of Africa had been carved up amongst the European powers, who had agreed amongst themselves on 'spheres of influence' at the Congress of Berlin (1878).
Left: Zulu warriors in South Africa were formidable fighters, but no match for the guns and rifles of the colonial forces.

British
French
German
Belgian
Italian
Portuguese
Spanish
Independent

An Age of Invention

At the end of the 1900s a wave of inventions changed many people's way of life. Electricity was harnessed and brought into people's homes. The first cars rattled along the roads. Soon people would fly the first flying machines.

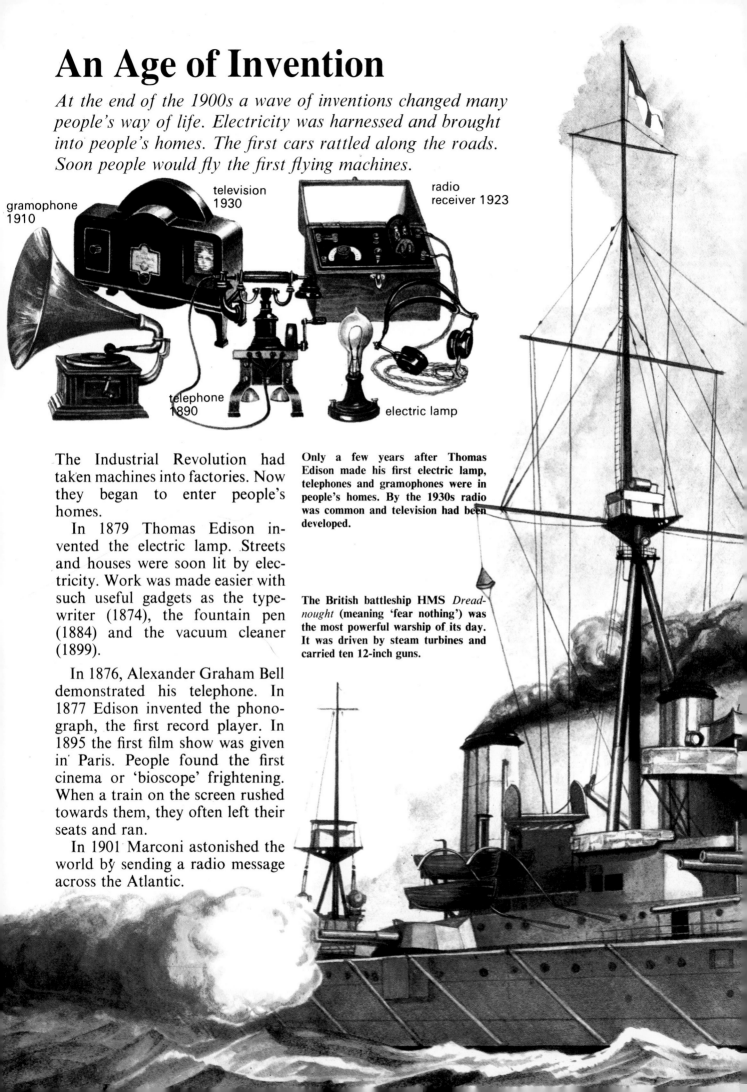

gramophone 1910

television 1930

radio receiver 1923

telephone 1890

electric lamp

The Industrial Revolution had taken machines into factories. Now they began to enter people's homes.

In 1879 Thomas Edison invented the electric lamp. Streets and houses were soon lit by electricity. Work was made easier with such useful gadgets as the typewriter (1874), the fountain pen (1884) and the vacuum cleaner (1899).

In 1876, Alexander Graham Bell demonstrated his telephone. In 1877 Edison invented the phonograph, the first record player. In 1895 the first film show was given in Paris. People found the first cinema or 'bioscope' frightening. When a train on the screen rushed towards them, they often left their seats and ran.

In 1901 Marconi astonished the world by sending a radio message across the Atlantic.

Only a few years after Thomas Edison made his first electric lamp, telephones and gramophones were in people's homes. By the 1930s radio was common and television had been developed.

The British battleship HMS *Dreadnought* (meaning 'fear nothing') was the most powerful warship of its day. It was driven by steam turbines and carried ten 12-inch guns.

Machines for Good and Ill

Discoveries such as X-rays (first used to take photographs inside the body in 1895), and radium (1898) were of great benefit to medicine. But science also brought terrible weapons of war. The automatic machine gun (1889) could kill dozens of people a minute. From 1906 powerful battleships, called 'Dreadnoughts' were built. They were armor-plated, had huge guns and were driven by the fast steam turbine engine (1894).

Farther and Faster

On December 17, 1903, the Wright brothers made their first short powered flight over the sands of Kitty Hawk, North Carolina. The age of the airplane had begun.

On land, the horse was being replaced by the 'horseless carriage'. Because cars were thought to be so dangerous, a man on foot often went ahead carrying a red flag as a warning.

But, in a few years, motor cars were a common sight on the roads of America and Europe. And airplanes were developed so rapidly that, in 1909, Louis Bleriot flew across the English Channel.

The new inventions made life easier, faster, more exciting, and more dangerous. The slow-moving, settled 1800s had given way to the fast-changing 20th Century—the age of technology.

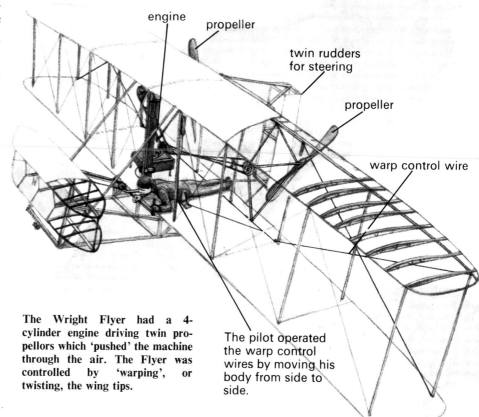

engine   propeller

twin rudders for steering

propeller

warp control wire

The Wright Flyer had a 4-cylinder engine driving twin propellors which 'pushed' the machine through the air. The Flyer was controlled by 'warping', or twisting, the wing tips.

The pilot operated the warp control wires by moving his body from side to side.

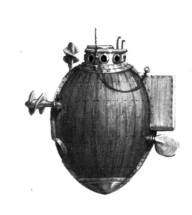

THE SUBMARINE

The first military submarine was this strange American craft. It was built for one man and was screw-propelled. In 1776 the tiny machine was used to try to sink a British man-of-war in New York harbor by screwing explosive charges onto the wooden hull. It was not until the 1890s that practicable submarines were developed. In 1898, an American submarine was launched. In 1900 it was commissioned in the American Navy as the U.S.S. *Holland* (after its inventor John P. Holland).

To the Poles

The North and South Poles provided natural targets for explorers, and right at the end of the nineteenth century people began planning expeditions to tackle the perilous journeys. Appallingly cold conditions, blinding snow storms, treacherous crevasses, and even polar bears, had to be faced. And, at the end, tragedy struck at the South Pole, where a bitter race was finally won by a Norwegian.

Reaching the North Pole

The first person to make an attempt to reach the North Pole was a Norwegian called Nansen. He knew that the frozen ice of the Arctic did not stay still but drifted slowly, pushed by the ocean currents, from east to west. So anything frozen into the ice would be carried with it westwards. He therefore equipped a specially built ship, with strong sides so the pressure of the ice would not crush it, and set out from the most northerly point of Siberia in June 1893.

The plan worked and Nansen's ship was pushed up onto the ice and began to drift slowly westwards. But after a year Nansen realized that the ship was going to miss the North Pole. With one companion, he set out on foot and met every sort of difficulty. They were nearly killed by a surprise attack from a polar bear. Exhausted, and with 200 miles to go, Nansen had to turn back.

Another Norwegian called Amundsen decided to take up the challenge, but before he could start, he learned that an American, Robert Peary, had already reached the Pole. Having no scientific interest in the Pole, Peary had traveled lightly and at great speed. He dashed across the ice on a sledge and reached the Pole on April 6, 1909. Amundsen's interest turned to the South Pole.

The Race to the South Pole

Another expedition had already been planned. On November 27, 1910, a British party under the leadership of Robert Scott, had set off from Dunedin, New Zealand, in a ship, the *Terra Nova*, which was crammed with stores and equipment. There were 33 Husky dogs, 19

Roald Amundsen plants the Norwegian flag at the South Pole. Having been beaten to the North Pole, Amundsen was determined to be the first to the South Pole. For the journey he set up only three depots and built light sledges to travel over the ice. On the treacherous Axel Heiburg Glacier he lost 10 dogs in a crevasse and then had to shoot 24 of the weakest surviving to provide the rest of the expedition with food. When he reached the Pole he left a message for Scott who arrived a month later. His victory dealt a dreadful blow to the British party's morale. Amundsen himself got back safely to the Bay of Whales on January 25, 1912. He disappeared in an Arctic expedition in 1930.

Mongolian ponies for hauling the sledges and 60 men. After terrible storms they landed in Antarctica at Hurrah Beach. One motor sledge sank through the ice as it was being unloaded and killer whales were responsible for the deaths of three ponies. Nevertheless, the crew were cheerful as they began to build a base and to set out depots along the route to the Pole. After a year on the ice nine depots had been established. Five men set out to make the final assault.

Meanwhile, Amundsen had decided to beat Scott to the Pole. He landed 70 miles nearer the Pole than Scott's base, and, making a quick dash, reached the goal on December 15, 1911.

Unaware of Amundsen's victory, Scott plowed on. When his party finally reached the Pole they were shattered to discover a Norwegian flag and a message from Amundsen. Dejected, they started out on the return trip. The journey back was even worse than it had been on the way out. They had expected hard ice, but instead clinging snow slowed them down. Gradually, their strength faded and they covered less and less ground each day. Their food was running out and one man, Evans, died. Another, Oates, disappeared in the snow. Within days Scott and the other two had also died, only eleven miles from a depot.

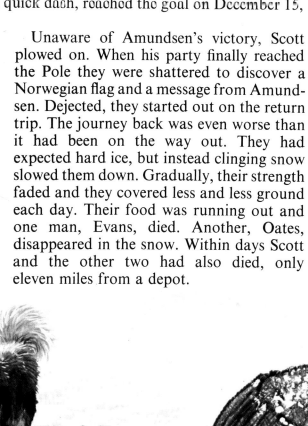

The End of an Era

Victoria was the longest reigning monarch in British history. During the 64 years that she was Queen, Britain had become the most powerful nation in the world. But, as she celebrated her Jubilee in 1897, there were already signs that things were changing. Rivalry from other European nations was shortly to explode into the most terrible war the world had ever experienced.

During the 18th and 19th centuries Great Britain had acquired an Empire that covered a quarter of the world's land surface. Having established a military presence in each of its territories in India, the Far East, Australia and Africa, Britain assured itself of ready access to huge markets for exporting manufactured goods. This imperialism when combined with coal and steel production that far outstripped that of other nations contributed to Britain's preeminence in trade.

European Rivalry

But in many ways, as Prime Minister Disraeli had said, the Empire was a millstone around Britain's neck. Administrators had to be sent to every part of the dominions and soldiers had to be ready to quell increasing outbreaks of unrest. This was a drain on resources and a distraction from making improvements at home that were urgently needed. It also led to complacency, and to a feeling that the British were supreme. This, not unnaturally, caused annoyance among European rivals.

Germany, especially, was determined to show its equality with Britain. Quickly, it stepped up production of raw materials and ship building to challenge Britain's supremacy at sea. In Africa, Germany was in the forefront of the European nations eager to establish colonies on that continent.

Suspicious of the power build-up of its neighbor to the east, France nervously began to look for friends. In 1904 Britain and France came to a mutual understanding called the *Entente Cordiale*. Two decades earlier, Germany had reached agreements with Austria-Hungary and Italy. Europe was splitting into two camps.

At the same time these countries were forming alliances, their economies were suffering. Many Europeans were forced by circumstances to emigrate to other countries, the United States in particular, to start life afresh, far from poverty, famine, political oppression, and rumors of war.

Right: This painting, entitled 'The Last of England', shows a dejected young couple setting out from home to start a new life overseas. It is clear from the sorrowful expressions on their faces that they do not want to go; but economic and social conditions in Europe during the 19th century forced emigration on millions of people just like them. In the 1840s the potato famine in Ireland forced thousands of people to leave their homes and search for a better life elsewhere. Behind the pomp and magnificence of Empire the lives of ordinary people were often wretched. In desperation they looked to the colonies and to the United States where they could prosper as a result of their own efforts.

Below: This typewriter, made in 1876, might be a symbol of the growing expansion of commerce in the late nineteenth century. Offices were changing as business expanded.

Below: On June 22, 1897 Queen Victoria celebrated her Diamond Jubilee. Dressed in black and shaded from the bright sun by an umbrella, she rode from Buckingham Palace to St. Paul's in an open carriage waving to the crowds who lined the route. Behind her was a procession of soldiers from all over the Empire including princes from India, tribesmen from Africa, troopers from Australia, Cypriots in fezzes and Chinese in straw hats.

The Motor Car

The invention of the internal combustion engine had profound effects on the world at the turn of the century. With the coming of mass production, private car ownership became a reality and hundreds of miles of roadway had to be built for the new vehicles.

Left: A steam tractor built by the French engineer Nicolas Cugnot in 1769. It was designed to haul cannon and was heavy and awkward. Nevertheless, it is regarded as the first true motor vehicle. Later engineers attempted to improve on the design, but it was not until the invention of the internal combustion engine that efficient powered road transport was possible.

Before the motor car was invented several attempts had been made to perfect a steam-powered vehicle suitable for the roads. All had been noisy, slow and inefficient. Until the end of the 19th century, therefore, all road vehicles, apart from the bicycle, had been horse-drawn. In large cities the roads became jammed with carriages and the noise from the clatter of iron-shod wheels on cobbles could be deafening. In addition there could be a strong smell from horse droppings when it was hot. Children could earn a few pennies by sweeping crossings for pedestrians or holding the bridles of waiting horses.

Above: Gottlieb Daimler's first motor car, which he produced in Germany in 1886. Early cars such as this were very similar to horse carriages fitted with engines. They had wheels like those on carts or bicycles and folding hoods or no hoods at all. A tiller was used to steer the car and the wheels were driven by a system of belts. Starting the engine often involved lighting a hot tube ignition burner and trimming and adjusting a wick in the carburetor.
Below: An early Rolls Royce Silver Shadow, the result of high quality engineering and superb design, brought luxury and comfort to road travel. Needless to say, cars such as this were very expensive.

The Bicycle Craze
The first bicycle to be invented was called a 'boneshaker' for obvious reasons. It had wooden wheels and iron tires and was very bumpy to ride. Then came the 'high-wheeler' which had a huge front wheel and small back wheel, making it both difficult and dangerous to ride. The pedals were fixed to the front hub. 'Stanley's safety cycle' was invented in 1885 and had equal-sized wheels and chain drive. Suddenly everyone took to this novel way of getting around. But the craze was not to last long. In the same year that Stanley produced his machine Karl Benz in Germany had invented the first motor car using an internal combustion engine that used gasoline. This was to herald a new transport age.

Early Motor Cars

Benz's car was a light three-wheeler. Gottlieb Daimler's car, which followed the next year, was merely a four-wheeled carriage from which the shafts had been removed and which had an engine fitted. The first 'modern' car, with the engine at the front under a hood, a gearbox, a foot-controlled clutch and rear wheel drive, was the Panhard-Levassor of 1891. Louis Renault, a French engineer, built the first fully enclosed car in 1898. He also invented the drive shaft.

Mass Production

In 1903 Ransom Eli Olds made the first mass-produced car—the Oldsmobile 'Curved Dash' buggy. Production lines were established and cars were assembled in volume. But it was not until Henry Ford started producing his Model T that prices came tumbling down. Suddenly cars were no longer the preserve of only the very rich. Within years cities had traffic jams of cars and not horses.

Over the decades since its first appearance, the motor car developed from a 'horseless carriage'

into a streamlined automobile. The steering wheel replaced a stick called the tiller, air-filled tires replaced solid ones, and the ride became smoother.

However, despite these improvements, a practical replacement for the gasoline-powered engine has not yet been developed. Today, periodic fuel shortages caused by unrest in the Middle East, where most of the world's oil is produced, have prompted fuel conservation in the United States and elsewhere.

Car Racing

As car design improved, so did speed. The first auto race was held in 1895. A round trip between Paris and Bordeaux, France, it covered over 800 miles. The winner's time was nearly 49 hours, his car averaging 15 mph.

Eventually, auto racing developed into an exciting international sport, with Grand Prix races held in most major countries, including the U.S., France, Great Britain, and nations as diverse as Argentina, Sweden, and Japan. In these races *Formula 1* cars race by at speeds of up to 200 mph.

Henry Ford produced his first car, the Quadricycle in 1896 in Detroit. Twelve years later he began mass-producing a car called the Model T. 15 million of these were to be sold by the time that production ceased in 1927. Mass production brought the price of motoring within the range of far larger numbers.

The Story of Aircraft

People have always longed to fly like birds. It was not until this century that this ambition could be achieved.

Over the ages many men have tried to fit themselves with wings and fly. But people cannot keep themselves up using their own muscles to flap wings.

The Chinese were flying kites before 200 BC. From finding out what made kites fly, people began to build

The Wright brothers make the first-ever powered flight.

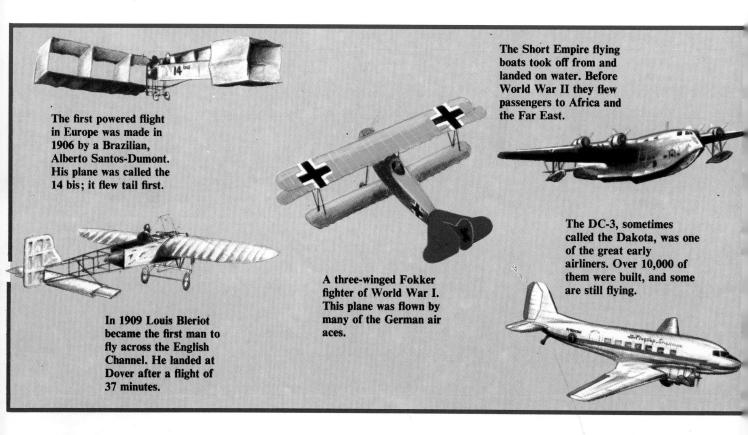

The first powered flight in Europe was made in 1906 by a Brazilian, Alberto Santos-Dumont. His plane was called the 14 bis; it flew tail first.

In 1909 Louis Bleriot became the first man to fly across the English Channel. He landed at Dover after a flight of 37 minutes.

A three-winged Fokker fighter of World War I. This plane was flown by many of the German air aces.

The Short Empire flying boats took off from and landed on water. Before World War II they flew passengers to Africa and the Far East.

The DC-3, sometimes called the Dakota, was one of the great early airliners. Over 10,000 of them were built, and some are still flying.

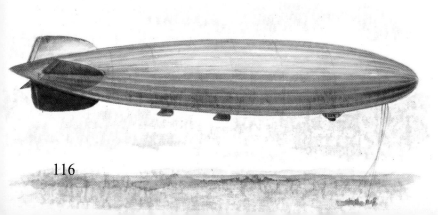

During the 18th century, the French Montgolfier brothers first flew in hot air balloons. Later, men filled balloons with hydrogen gas instead of heated air. From 1850, people tried to fit balloons with engines and propellers, so that they could be steered— the first airships. The greatest airship designer was the German Count von Zeppelin. He made many huge airships during World War I: some dropped bombs on England. After the war, big 'Zeppelins' carried passengers across the oceans. But when the Zeppelin company's 'Hindenburg' exploded, killing 36 people, that was the end of the monster airships.

gliders. The American brothers Orville and Wilbur Wright worked with gliders. On December 17, 1903 they took a machine similar to a glider but with a gasoline engine to the coastal dunes of Kitty Hawk, North Carolina. Orville flew the strange machine for 12 seconds. This was the first of four successful flights that day of powered aircraft. The principles developed by the Wright brothers are used in every aircraft that flies today.

In 1909 a Frenchman, Louis Blériot, became the first man to fly across the English Channel. The flight took 37 minutes.

During World War I, 1914-1918, pilots adapted their planes to fight each other in the air, and to drop bombs. In 1927 the first one-man crossing of the Atlantic was made by the American Charles Lindbergh in a grueling 33 hours—with no radio or parachute! World War II, 1939-1945, saw the first flight of famous warplanes like the British Spitfire and the German Me-109. Later in the war, the first jet plane appeared.

Today ordinary people fly all over the world—quite a step from Orville Wright's 12-second flight of 1903!

The German Otto Lilienthal learned about flying by making gliders. He hung below his early machines and controlled them by swinging his body. He was nearly ready to fit an engine to his strange craft when he crashed and was killed.

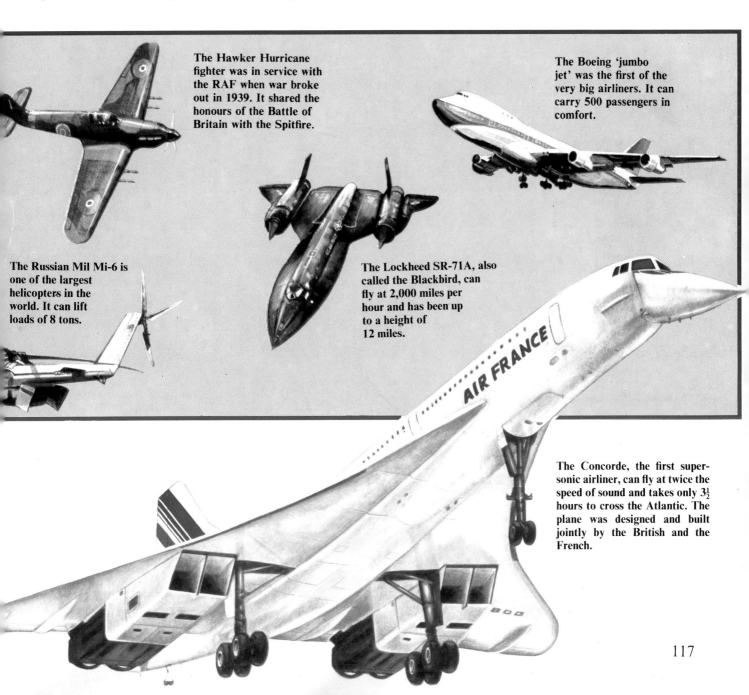

The Hawker Hurricane fighter was in service with the RAF when war broke out in 1939. It shared the honours of the Battle of Britain with the Spitfire.

The Boeing 'jumbo jet' was the first of the very big airliners. It can carry 500 passengers in comfort.

The Russian Mil Mi-6 is one of the largest helicopters in the world. It can lift loads of 8 tons.

The Lockheed SR-71A, also called the Blackbird, can fly at 2,000 miles per hour and has been up to a height of 12 miles.

The Concorde, the first super-sonic airliner, can fly at twice the speed of sound and takes only $3\frac{1}{2}$ hours to cross the Atlantic. The plane was designed and built jointly by the British and the French.

The Great War

The murder of Archduke Francis Ferdinand of Austria by a Serbian in June 1914 helped to start World War I.

The Great War of 1914–1918, now known as World War I, was fought by most of the world's great nations. People were horrified by this new kind of warfare and the terrible destruction it caused.

In August 1914, when World War I began, thousands of men (Germans, Austrians, and Turks on one side; British, French and Russians on the other) rushed to join the armed forces. People sang and cheered as the soldiers marched off to fight.

By the end of 1914 this mood of cheerful patriotism had changed. People were shocked and afraid; no one had realized that modern warfare would be so devastating in destruction of lives and property. The war they thought would end quickly was to last four years.

'dogfights' in the air

During World War I many new machines and kinds of equipment were tested and used in war for the first time.

gas mask

ambulance

The Machines of War

Both sides had guns so powerful that they could fire shells for hours on end, destroying everything within range. Many battles began with huge artillery 'barrages'. When the guns stopped firing, all that was left was a sea of mud and ruins. A single machine gun could slaughter dozens of men in minutes. Armies could not move forward against such guns. So they dug themselves lines of trenches. The trenches protected soldiers from gunfire, but not from poison gas.

This was the first war in which men fought in the air. Pilots in light, fragile planes fired at each other with pistols and machine guns. They had no parachutes, so could not escape if their planes were shot down.

Tanks were first used in 1916 by the British. The Germans were terrified to see these crawling 'tin boxes' and ran away. At sea, many merchant ships were sunk by submarines, lurking unseen beneath the water.

'The War to End All Wars'

It was the submarines' success in sinking unarmed ships that prompted U.S. President Woodrow Wilson to ask Congress for a declaration of war against Germany. In June 1917 American soldiers began pouring into France to reinforce the war-weary Allied troops. By the time 2 million American soldiers had landed in France, the war was drawing to a close. Less than two years after Wilson's declaration, the German government signed an armistice treaty.

Over 10 million soldiers had been killed. Never before had there been such death and destruction. Everyone hoped it was 'the war to end all wars.' It was not. A war even more terrible lay ahead.

Far left: 'Your country needs you' was the message on this recruiting poster. At first, men joined the army eagerly. But when the horrors of trench warfare (left) became known, people changed their minds about the so-called 'glory' of war.

Right: Zeppelin airships flew to Britain and dropped bombs.

Between Two Wars

The generation who had lived through the Great War was determined to enjoy the prosperity of the 1920s. But unemployment, caused by the Great Depression, and Hitler's rise to power soon dampened their enthusiasm.

The immediate outcome of the Great War was a determination among the victors that such a conflict should be avoided in future, and that Germany should be made to pay for her aggression. To achieve the first aim the League of Nations was set up in order to promote international cooperation and to maintain the peace.

Germany was made to suffer heavily under the terms of the Treaty of Versailles (1919). Massive compensation was to be paid to the Allies, and her colonies and some of her territories were forfeited. In fact Germany did not pay most of the 'reparations', but her people felt humiliated and avidly supported Hitler when he came to power, determined to throw off the stigma of war guilt. The League of Nations proved to be a powerless organization whose protests and threats were ignored by Italy and Germany.

Hitler began to amass huge armies. He took back coalfields that had been confiscated at Versailles. Europe stood by as he marched into Austria and Czechoslovakia. Resistance came, however, when he attacked Poland in 1939.

Early versions of machines in common use today bear little resemblance to their modern counterparts.

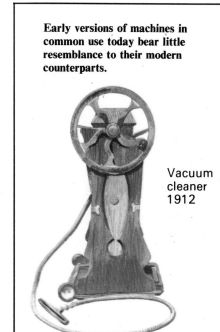

Vacuum cleaner 1912

Washing machine 1920

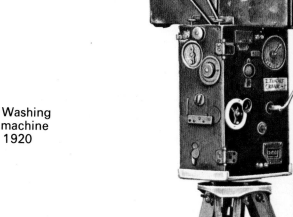

Hand-cranked movie camera 1920

The Roaring 'Twenties and the Great Depression

Relief that the Great War was over exploded on both sides of the Atlantic into a decade during which people were determined to enjoy themselves. In the United States, the exciting rhythms of jazz were everywhere. Women had just won the right to vote. And despite Prohibition, outlawing the production and consumption of alcohol, bootleggers kept liquor in abundant supply. Life seemed to be one long party as speakeasies, sports stadiums, and movie houses overflowed.

Prosperity was the keynote until one day, late in October 1929. Prices on the New York Stock Exchange plummeted, signalling the beginning of the Great Depression. Factories, mines, and offices closed as Americans became increasingly unable to pay for goods and services. Millions were without work, and money was scarce. When banks failed, rioting broke out among people who were denied access to savings and investments that no longer existed.

In 1932 Franklin D. Roosevelt was elected President of the United States. In his first term he announced a New Deal that created various government agencies to combat the country's desperate economic situation. He initiated legislation to regulate banks, help farmers, enforce fairness in business, and create work for the unemployed. Still, economic recovery was painfully slow. And in the background was the increasing threat to peace caused by the rise of fascist regimes in Germany and Italy.

In New York office and apartment blocks were built upwards because land was scarce and therefore valuable. Soon the main part of the city was full of 'skyscrapers'. In Europe such buildings were not constructed until after World War II when a lot of reconstruction work had to be done in the bombed cities.

During the inter-war years great strides forward were made in technology. Engineers, scientists and mechanics made significant advances in the design of machines that had already been invented, like the motor car and the motorcycle. Although airplanes had been used in the Great War, air transport was still in its infancy in 1918. During the next 20 years many improvements were made. Engines became more reliable and stronger, and aircraft frames bigger and sturdier. By the outbreak of World War II there were some very sophisticated planes. In the home, machines like the vacuum cleaner and washing machine began to make life easier. For entertainment people could listen to the 'wireless' and, by the mid 30s, television had been invented—though few, as yet, could watch it.

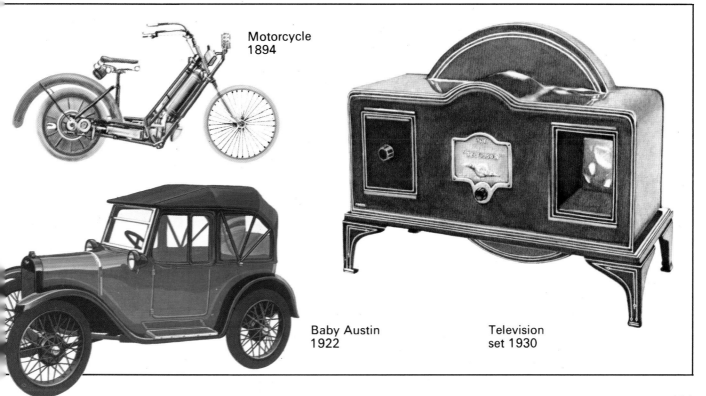

Motorcycle 1894

Baby Austin 1922

Television set 1930

The World at War

World War II was the first war to be fought around the world, from the baking deserts of Africa to the snowy plains of Russia, from the air to deep under the sea.

World War II began when Britain and France declared war on Nazi Germany on September 3rd, 1939. Nine months later Italy declared war on France and Britain. Gradually, nations aligned themselves either with the Axis or the Allies: The chief powers of the Axis were Germany, Italy, and Japan. By 1941 the chief powers of the Allies were the U.S., Great Britain and Russia.

World War II involved not only soldiers, sailors and airmen, but also millions of ordinary civilians. Many Europeans became conquered peoples when between 1939 and 1941 the Nazi armies occupied Poland, Norway, Denmark, the Netherlands, Belgium, France, Yugoslavia, and Greece. In these countries and in Russia millions of men and women were taken from their homes to become slave workers in Germany. Millions of Jews, gypsies, Communists and others whom the Nazis and their *Fuhrer* (leader) Adolf Hitler hated were put into concentration camps. Most, including six million Jews, died there.

Threat from the Air
Between July and October 1940, in the Battle of Britain, the Royal Air Force defeated the German *Luftwaffe* (air force). Hitler had to give up his plans to invade Britain. But night after night Luftwaffe planes bombed British towns and cities.

The United States Enters the War
On December 7, 1941 the Japanese launched a surprise attack and bombed Pearl Harbor, Hawaii. More than 2,400 military personnel and civilians were killed in that raid, and over 1,000 were wounded. A major portion of the U.S. Pacific naval fleet was destroyed.

President Roosevelt asked Congress for a declaration of war against Japan. Days later the United States was at war with Germany and Italy as well.

As 'the great arsenal of democracy,' the United States had kept the Allies supplied with food and war materials since the beginning of the war. Now that U.S. involvement was official, millions of American fighting men were sent to Europe to fight the Axis.

D-Day

On June 6, 1944, U.S. and British forces landed on the beaches of Normandy, France and fought their way across the continent into the heart of Nazi Germany. There they were joined by the Russians from the east. On May 8, 1945 the Germans surrendered.

In Asia and the Pacific the war continued. Gradually, the Allies captured one Japanese-held island after another, but many lives were lost in the process. Then, in an effort to bring the war to an end, the U.S. sent a B-29 bomber to drop an atomic bomb on the Japanese city of Hiroshima. Three days later Nagasaki was partly destroyed by another atomic bomb. Nearly 100,000 people were killed, and as many injured. This action prompted the Japanese to surrender on September 2, 1945, and World War II was over.

Left: The attack on Pearl Harbor brought the United States into World War II.

In the North African desert war British tanks under General Bernard Montgomery (below left) pushed back the Germans, led by General Erwin Rommel (below right).

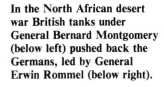

The Cold War and Beyond

At the end of World War II, the United States and the Soviet Union emerged as the strongest nations in the world. Though the world hoped for peace, ideological differences between these and other countries led to further conflicts.

In the decades following World War II, another kind of war was taking shape — the 'cold war.' On one side was the Soviet Union and its communist satellites; on the other, the United States and the 'free world.' Though these two superpowers never met head-on in military action, the tension generated by their contrasting systems of government often formed the background for conflicts in other countries. But, given the development of atomic weapons, people began to question the viability of war as a way to resolve differences.

On October 24, 1945 the United Nations was established to promote world peace and to guarantee human dignity. An organization made up of representatives from nearly every country, the UN was instrumental in either avoiding or bringing to an end a number of conflicts. In the Middle East, the UN arranged cease-fires between the Arabs and Israelis several times since 1948, often supplying peacekeeping forces to prevent border violations. In Korea (1950–53), UN international troops under U.S. direction fought North Korean forces that had invaded South Korea.

During the 1960–70s peace advocacy became more widespread when U.S. involvement in the Vietnam War was viewed with disfavor by many at home, giving rise to anti-war protests. Today, the United States and the Soviet Union recognize the importance of arms control though they differ on ways to limit the arms race.

Above: A United Nations peacekeeping force on duty in one of the world's trouble spots. After the Second World War the League of Nations was disbanded and replaced by a stronger body which would represent every nation in the world. It has not prevented wars, but it has managed to bring them to an end on some occasions. Several UN agencies also do important work. Some encourage the development of education and technology, especially in the poorer countries. The World Health Organization works to improve medicine and curb disease.

Right: Artificial satellites stay in space for long periods of time, orbiting the earth. The weather satellite pictured here radios to Earth information that is used by forecasters to predict short- and long-term weather patterns. Other satellites are used specifically for communications, navigation, scientific experiments or information-gathering, or military purposes.

THE THIRD WORLD

The Third World is the name given to the developing countries of Africa, South America and Asia. Many of these countries were still colonies at the end of World War II but they have since gained their independence. This new-found freedom, however, did not automatically trigger immediate economic and technological advancement. Industries had to be started and technicians had to be trained to use complicated and expensive machinery. Farming methods were often out of date and hospitals and schools were badly needed. Gradually, though, these countries began to modernize and to take advantage of the raw materials they possessed. Some countries, for example, built thriving economies around oil exploration. These strong economies then supported full-scale educational systems for all school-age children. But, by and large, the Third World countries are still extremely poor in comparison to the richer industrial countries. They suffer too from political instability, poor harvests and widespread disease.

Left: At schools in Africa reading is taught to young and old alike. Education is still a priority in most Third World countries.

Quality of Life

Despite the political instability and military conflicts that continued to plague the postwar world, much was done to improve the quality of life. Though the disparity between rich and poor nations was still great, modern conveniences and medicine were becoming more available to everyone. Advances in science virtually eliminated such diseases as smallpox, contributed to the development of vaccines to prevent polio and other serious illnesses, and stimulated research into ways to treat cancer.

An explosion of technological achievement culminated in space exploration while contributing to improved lifestyles for millions of people the world over.

Many of the technological advancements that affected people's daily lives resulted, in fact, from the space program, which was undergoing vigorous development at this time. As man pushed his influence out into space, first with artificial satellites and unmanned rockets, later in manned space flights, his discoveries led to improved global communications, transportation, and weather forecasting. Unfortunately, this influence carries with it man's problems and conflicts, including the potential of war on a far grander scale than ever before.

The collage on the left gives an impression of what has been achieved in the short time since space exploration began. It started on October 4, 1957 when the Russians launched an artificial satellite, called *Sputnik I*, into orbit around the Earth. Soon afterwards a small dog called Laika became the first living creature to travel in space. Two months later the United States launched its first satellite, *Explorer I*, and the space race was on.

The first man to travel in space was a Russian called Yuri Gagarin. He made a single orbit of the Earth in April 1961. The United States decided that its first priority would be to put a man on the Moon.

But other achievements went on at the same time. In 1962 the U.S. launched *Telstar*, the first communications satellite. This acted as an aerial which could bounce radio and television signals from one side of the world to the other. This was followed by a weather satellite that sent back pictures to Earth showing cloud formations and tropical storms. Developed from this was the spy satellite. It could show troop movements and even warn if missiles were being launched by an enemy.

Manned space flights continued throughout the 1960s and 1970s. In June 1965, Edward White made the first space-walk, outside his space capsule. The following year the first space-link took place. This opened up the way for the assembly of large units in space. One such unit was *Skylab*. It was 118 ft. (36 meters) long and fitted with telescopes, cameras and other equipment. With such structures it was possible for men to stay in space for months. Here, clockwise from top left: the Earth seen from space; *Skylab;* a space station; a satellite; a lunar module; a Russian cosmonaut; an American walking on the Moon's surface; and a giant rocket.

The Journey to the Moon

The Moon has always fascinated people, and the successful launch of rockets beyond the pull of the Earth's gravity meant that the dream of putting a person on the Moon was at last a possibility.

In 1961 President Kennedy said: "I believe that this nation should commit itself to achieving the goal, before this decade is out, of landing a man successfully on the Moon and returning him safely to Earth."

In 1969 his declaration was fulfilled.

The preparations for the Moon landing were called the *Apollo* program. Mounted on huge *Saturn V* rockets, a series of *Apollo* spacecraft were launched. The program began with a disaster. While carrying out routine tests in the *Apollo 1* capsule, three astronauts (Grissom, White and Chaffee) were killed in a fire caused by an electrical fault. Three months later a Russian, Victor Komarov, was killed when a problem sent his spacecraft hurtling back into the Earth's atmosphere much faster than was intended. His spacecraft burned up in the intense heat.

Despite these tragedies work went ahead, and in December 1968 *Apollo 8* made ten orbits of the Moon and returned safely to Earth. *Apollo 10*, in May 1969, was the dress rehearsal for the final assault. All went well and two months later *Apollo 11* was launched.

The crew of three was commanded by Neil Armstrong. He was to be accompanied on the Moon landing by "Buzz" Aldrin, while the third man, Michael Collins, was to remain orbiting the Moon in the command module.

The launch on July 16 went without a hitch. At Mission Control in Houston, Texas, hundreds of people watched the rocket's progress. Huge computers set the spacecraft on a course for the Moon. 70 miles above the Moon's surface, Collins put the two parts of the craft, *Eagle* and *Columbia*, into orbit. All was set for the landing. *Eagle* was launched from the command module and eventually landed at a spot called "Tranquillity Base". "The *Eagle* has landed," reported Armstrong.

Since this first landing, astronauts have stepped onto the moon's surface several times. During the 1970s, however, interest in other planets prompted the launching of unmanned, information-gathering rockets, such as the Mariner and Viking missions to Mars in 1971 and 1976, respectively. At the same time both the United States and the Soviet Union sent up orbiting space stations—Skylab (US) and Salyut (USSR). The most recent missions into space involve the space shuttle, first launched in 1981. It is different from all prior spacecraft because it can return to earth under a pilot's control and be reused.

Above: A lunar module descending onto the pitted surface of the Moon.
Left: The space shuttle has shed its booster rockets and external fuel tank and is floating in orbit. It is seen launching a large satellite by means of its remote-controlled manipulating arm. Its voluminous cargo bay can carry loads 60 feet long and 15 feet across.

Right: Its mission completed, the shuttle reenters the atmosphere and glides to a runway landing. Within two weeks it will be ready to return to orbit.

Tomorrow's World

Predictions about the future should only be made with a great deal of caution since unforeseen changes can quickly upset the most likely developments. Some of the changes described below may never happen; others will already have happened by the time you read this.

Man has already been to the Moon and stayed in space for months on end. Rockets have traveled deep into space to photograph other planets and it is possible that manned voyages will also take place. Certainly, massive space stations are only just around the corner. These will be used as bases for other craft and as telecommunications centers.

On Earth, supersonic passenger planes will become more common and it will be possible to travel farther much faster. Because the world supply of oil will eventually run out, the days of the motor car in its present form are numbered. No one yet knows what will take its place since so far experiments with electrically powered cars have not proved economical. Travel by sea is likely to remain much the same, though increasing use may be made of sails to help power huge tankers.

Alternative Energy Sources

A great deal of work is already being done to find energy sources that are not dependent on dwindling natural reserves. Oil has even been extracted from rotting rubbish. The most likely sources of energy are, however, the sun, the wind and the sea. Huge solar panels can be built on the roofs of houses to capture the sun's rays and store their energy. Large windmills can generate electricity. Massive booms stretched across the estuaries of rivers can also transform wave movement into electricity. In addition, there is nuclear power already being used to provide a large proportion of the West's energy requirements.

The Computer Revolution

Now that the world has entered the age of the computer, there is hardly an aspect of life left unaffected. Ever since the tiny silicon chip replaced the transistor, computers have become increasingly compact and far more accessible than ever before. In industry, for example, programmable robots have eliminated human involvement in many risky or tedious tasks. Many households have their own personal home computers, regarding them as much a necessity as a radio, television, or stereo system. Soon it may be possible to do the shopping at home using a personal computer.

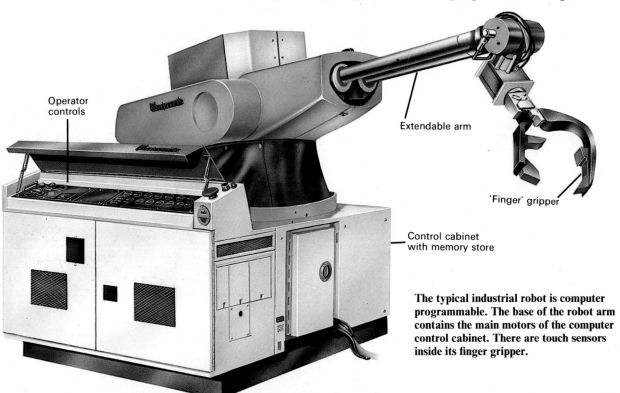

Operator controls

Extendable arm

'Finger' gripper

Control cabinet with memory store

The typical industrial robot is computer programmable. The base of the robot arm contains the main motors of the computer control cabinet. There are touch sensors inside its finger gripper.

Space colonies like this are being considered as alternatives to cities on Earth. This one is a torus habitat controlled by a huge central computer. It consists of a tube 430 feet across that forms a ring a mile in diameter. The tube houses the main living and agricultural areas of the colony and can support up to 10,000 people. From the outside the habitat looks like a big wheel with a hub at the center (above). The tube rotates once a minute to create artificial gravity on the surface of the tube away from the hub. 'Up' is toward the hub and 'down' is away from it.

The hub houses solar power stations and docking facilities for spaceships. On it are mirrors to reflect sunlight to the living areas and to provide energy to drive the generators that produce the colony's electricity. Long 'spokes' attach the tube to the central hub.

What Happened in History

Different parts of the world developed at different times. Civilizations and empires rose and declined. Different peoples influenced the world at different times. A chronology, or list of dates arranged in order, shows us what was happening in different places at the same time and so gives us a bird's eye view of what happened in history.

EUROPE

BC

c 20,000	Cave paintings in France and Spain
c 6500	First farming in Greece
c 2600	Beginnings of Minoan civilization in Crete
c 1600	Beginnings of Mycenaean civilization in Greece
c 1450	Destruction of Minoan Crete
c 1200	Collapse of Mycenaean empire
c 1100	Phoenician supremacy in Mediterranean Sea
900-750	Rise of city-states in Greece
776	First Olympic Games
753	Foundation of Rome (traditional date)
510	Foundation of Roman Republic
477-405	Athenian supremacy in Aegean
431-404	War between Athens and Sparta
290	Roman conquest of central Italy
146	Greece comes under Roman domination
31	Battle of Actium. Octavian defeats Mark Antony

AD

43	Roman invasion of Britain
116	Emperor Trajan extends Roman Empire to Euphrates
238	Beginning of raids by Goths into Roman Empire

AMERICAS

BC

c 36,000	Neanderthal man reaches North America via Bering Strait land bridge
c 10,500	Man appears in South America
c 3000	First pottery in Mexico
c 2500	Farming begins in North America
c 2000	First metalworking in Peru

ASIA

BC

c 8000	Agriculture develops in the Middle East
c 6000	Rice cultivated in Thailand
c 4000	Bronze casting begins in Near East
c 3000	Development of major cities in Sumer
c 2750	Growth of civilizations in Indus Valley
c 2200	Hsia dynasty in China
c 1750	Collapse of Indus Valley civilization
c 1500	Rise of Shang dynasty in China
c 1200	Beginning of Jewish religion
c 1050	Shang dynasty overthrown by Chou in China
c 770	Chou dynasty is weakening
c 720	Height of Assyrian power
c 650	First iron used in China
586	Babylonian captivity of Jews
483-221	'Warring States' period in China
202	Han dynasty reunites China

AD

c 0	Buddhism introduced to China from India
25	Han dynasty restored in China
45	Beginning of St Paul's missionary journeys
132	Jewish rebellion against Rome
220	End of Han dynasty; China splits into three states

AFRICA	PEOPLE	INVENTIONS DISCOVERIES
BC		**BC**
c 5000 Agricultural settlements in Egypt		c 6000 First known pottery and textiles
	BC	c 5000 First known use of irrigation
	c 2650 Death of King Zoser of Egypt, for whom first pyramid was built	c 4000 Invention of plough and sail
c 3100 King Menes unites Egypt		c 3100 First known use of writing on clay tablets
c 2685 Beginning of 'Old Kingdom' in Egypt		c 2590 Cheops builds Great Pyramid at Giza in Egypt
	1792-50 Rule of Hammurabi in Babylon	
	1361-52 Rule of Tutankhamun in Egypt	
c 1570 Beginning of 'New Kingdom' in Egypt	1304-1237 Rule of Ramasses II in Egypt	
	1198-66 Reign of Ramasses III, last great Pharaoh	
		c 1100 Phoenicians develop alphabet
814 Carthage founded by Phoenicians		
	c 605-520 Lao-tzu, founder of Taoism	
	563-479 Siddhartha Gautama (the Buddha)	
	551-479 Confucius, Chinese thinker	
	427-347 Plato, Greek thinker	
	384-322 Aristotle, Greek thinker	
	356-323 Alexander the Great	
	100-44 Julius Caesar	
		c 214 Building of Great Wall of China
AD	**AD**	
30 Egypt becomes Roman province	63BC-14AD Augustus (Octavian), first Roman Emperor	**AD**
	54-68 Reign of Emperor Nero	142 First stone bridge built over River Tiber
	97-117 Reign of Emperor Trajan	
		c 105 First use of paper in China
		c 271 Magnetic compass in use in China

EUROPE		AMERICAS		ASIA	
		AD		**AD**	
293	Division of Roman Empire by Diocletian	c 300	Rise of Mayan civilization in Central America	330	Capital of Roman Empire transferred to Constantinople
370	Huns from Asia invade Europe			350	Huns invade Persia and India
410	Visigoths sack Rome				
449	Angles, Saxons and Jutes invade Britain	c 400	Beginnings of Incan civilization along South American Pacific coast	407-553	First Mongol Empire
486	Frankish kingdom founded by Clovis	c 455	Chichén Itzá founded by Mayans		
497	Franks converted to Christianity	c 600	Height of Mayan civilization	552	Buddhism introduced to Japan
				624	China re-united under T'ang dynasty
597	St. Augustine's mission to England			635	Muslims begin conquest of Syria and Persia
				674	Muslim conquest reaches River Indus
711	Muslim conquest of Spain				
732	Muslim advance halted at Battle of Poitiers				
				821	Conquest of Tibet by Chinese
793	Viking raids begin				
800	Charlemagne crowned Emperor in Rome				
843	Partition of Carolingian Empire at Treaty of Verdun				
874	First Viking settlers in Iceland				
886	King Alfred defeats Danish King Guthrum. Danelaw established in England				
911	Vikings granted duchy of Normandy by Frankish king	c 990	Expansion of Inca Empire	907	Last T'ang Emperor deposed in China
		c 1000	Leif Eriksson lands at Newfoundland	939	Civil wars in Japan
				979	Sung dynasty re-unites China
1016	King Cnut rules England, Denmark and Norway				
1066	William of Normandy defeats Anglo-Saxons at Hastings and becomes King of England			1054	Break between Greek and Latin Christian churches begins
1071	Normans conquer Byzantine Italy			1071	Seljuk Turks conquer most of Asia Minor
1095	Pope summons First Crusade				
		c 1100	Incan family under Manco Capac settle in Cuzco	c 1100	Polynesian Islands colonized
1147-9	Second Crusade	1151	End of Toltec Empire in Mexico	1156-89	Civil wars in Japan
1170	Murder of Thomas à Becket at Canterbury	1168	Aztecs leave Chimoztoc Valley	1174	Saladin conquers Syria
1189-92	Third Crusade			1187	Saladin captures Jerusalem
1198	Innocent III elected Pope			1190	Temujin begins to create Empire in Eastern Asia

AFRICA		PEOPLE		INVENTIONS DISCOVERIES	
		306–337	Reign of Emperor Constantine	c 300	Foot stirrup for riding invented
		340–420	St. Jerome, Bible translator		
		354–430	St. Augustine of Hippo		
		379–395	Theodosius I, Roman Emperor in the East		
429-535	Vandal kingdom in northern Africa				
533-552	Justinian restores Roman power in North Africa				
641	Conquest of Egypt by Muslims	480–543	St. Benedict, founder of first monastery		
c 700	Rise of Empire of Ghana			c 520	Rise of mathematics in India. Invention of decimal system
		527-565	Reign of Emperor Justinian		
		570-632	Muhammad, founder of Islam		
850	Acropolis of Zimbabwe built	590-604	Reign of Pope Gregory I		
		673-735	Venerable Bede, historian	c 730	First printing in China
				c 750	Paper-making spreads to Muslim world
		771-814	Reign of Charlemagne	760	Muslims adopt numerals
				788	Great Mosque built at Cordoba in Spain
				850	First printed book in China
				860	Discovery of Iceland by Vikings
920-1050	Height of Ghana Empire				
969	Fatamids conquer Egypt and found Cairo	987-996	Reign of Hugh Capet, first King of France	982	Erik the Red discovers Greenland
c 1000	First Iron Age settlement at Zimbabwe	980-1037	Avicenna, great Arab physician	c 1000	Vikings discover America
				c 1000	Great age of Chinese painting
		1066-1087	Reign of William I, King of England	c 1045	Moveable type printing invented in China
c 1150	Beginning of Yoruba city-states (Nigeria)	1138-93	Saladin, Sultan of Egypt and Syria	c 1100	Foundation of first universities in Europe
1174	Saladin conquers Egypt	1155-90	Reign of Emperor Frederick I	1161	Explosives used in China
c 1200	Rise of Empire of Mali in West Africa	1154-89	Reign of Henry II of England		
c 1200	Emergence of Hausa city-states (Nigeria)				

EUROPE

- **1202-1204** Fourth Crusade leads to capture of Constantinople and creation of Latin Empire
- **1215** King John of England signs Magna Carta
- **1217-1222** Fifth Crusade
- **1228-9** Sixth Crusade
- **1236** Mongols invade Russia
- **1241** Mongols invade Poland, Hungary, Bohemia, then withdraw
- **1248-70** Seventh Crusade
- **1250** Collapse of imperial power in Germany and Italy on death of Frederick II
- **1305** Papacy moves from Rome to Avignon
- **1312** Order of Knights Templars abolished
- **1337** Hundred Years' war begins between France and England
- **1346** English defeat French at Battle of Crecy
- **1348** Black Death reaches Europe
- **1356** English defeat French at Battle of Poitiers
- **1378-1417** Great Schism: (break between Rome and Avignon) rival popes elected
- **1381** Peasants' Revolt in England
- **1385** Independence of Portugal
- **1415** Henry V defeats French at Battle of Agincourt
- **1434** Cosimo de Medici becomes ruler of Florence
- **1453** England loses all French possessions except Calais
- **1455-85** Wars of the Roses in England
- **1459** Ottoman Turks conquer Serbia
- **1492** Last Muslims in Spain conquered by Christians
- **1517** Martin Luther nails 95 Theses to church door at Wittenberg
- **1519** Zwingli leads Reformation in Switzerland
- **1521** Luther condemned at Diet of Worms
- **1529** Reformation Parliament begins in England
- **1532** Calvin starts Protestant movement in France

AMERICAS

- **c 1300** Inca Roca takes title of Sapa Inca
- **1325** Rise of Aztecs. Founding of Tenochtitlan
- **1370** Expansion of Chimu kingdom
- **c 1375** Beginning of Aztec expansion
- **1438** Inca Empire established in Peru
- **1440–69** Ueue Montezuma rules Aztecs
- **1450** Incas conquer Chimu kingdom
- **1486–1502** Aztec Empire reaches sea
- **1492** Christopher Columbus reaches San Salvador
- **1493** Spanish establish first settlement in New World (Hispaniola)
- **1497** Amerigo Vespucci claims discovery of the New World. John Cabot lands at Newfoundland and Nova Scotia
- **1502–20** Aztec conquests under Montezuma II
- **c 1510** First African slaves taken to New World
- **1521** Cortes conquers Aztec capital, Tenochtitlan
- **1533** Pizzaro conquers Inca Empire
- **1535** Spaniards explore Chile

ASIA

- **1206** Temujin proclaimed Genghis Khan
- **1210** Mongols invade China
- **1234** Mongols destroy Chinese Empire
- **1261** Greek Empire restored at Constantinople
- **1279** Mongols conquer Southern China
- **1281** Mongols fail in attempt to conquer Japan
- **1299** Ottoman Turks begin expansion
- **c 1341** Black Death begins
- **1363** Tamerlane begins conquest of Asia
- **1368** Ming dynasty founded in China
- **1398** Tamerlane ravages kingdom of Delhi
- **1401** Tamerlane conquers Damascus and Baghdad
- **1402** Tamerlane overruns Ottoman Empire
- **1421** Peking becomes capital of China
- **1453** Ottoman Turks capture Constantinople
- **1516** Ottomans overrun Syria, Egypt and Arabia
- **1526** Foundation of Mughal Empire
- **1533** Ivan the Terrible succeeds to Russian throne

AFRICA		PEOPLE		INVENTIONS DISCOVERIES	
		1162–1227	Genghis Khan	1209	Foundation of Cambridge University in England
		1170–1221	St. Dominic, founder of Dominicans		
		1182–1226	St. Francis of Assisi, founder of Franciscans	1271-95	Journey to China by Marco Polo, father and uncle
		1214-1294	Roger Bacon, philosopher		
		1216-1294	Kublai Khan		
		1225-74	Thomas Aquinas, philosopher		
1240	Collapse of Empire of Ghana	1265-1321	Dante, Italian poet	1290	Spectacles invented in Italy
		1254-1324	Marco Polo, traveller		
		1276-1337	Giotto, Italian painter		
c 1300	Emergence of Ife Kingdom (West Africa)	1304-74	Petrarch, Italian poet		
		1320-84	John Wycliffe, religious reformer		
		1336-1405	Tamerlane, Mongol Emperor		
		1340-1400	Geoffrey Chaucer, English poet		
		1369-1415	John Huss, German religious reformer		
		1377-1446	Brunelleschi, Italian architect		
		1380-1471	Thomas à Kempis, German theologian	1405	Chinese voyages in the Indian Ocean
		1386-1466	Donatello, Italian sculptor		
				1445	Gutenberg prints first book from moveable type (in Europe)
		1394-1460	Henry the Navigator	1455	Cadamosto explores West Africa
		1412-31	Joan of Arc of France		
		1422-91	William Caxton, English printer	1488	Bartolomeo Diaz sails round Cape of Good Hope
		1444-1514	Bramante, Italian architect		
1415	Beginning of Portugal's African Empire	1451-1506	Christopher Columbus	1492	Columbus reaches West Indies
		1452-98	Savonarola, reformer	1497	John Cabot reaches Newfoundland
		1452-1519	Leonardo da Vinci		
1450	Height of Songhai Empire in West Africa	1460-1524	Vasco da Gama, explorer	1498	Vasco da Gama reaches India round Cape of Good Hope
		1466-1536	Erasmus, Renaissance writer		
1482	Portuguese settle Gold Coast (now Ghana)	1475-1564	Michelangelo, artist	1501	Vespucci explores Brazilian coast
		1470-1521	Fernando Magellan explorer	1509	Invention of watch
1492	Spain begins conquest of North African coast	1483-1520	Raphael, Renaissance painter	1522	Magellan's expedition completes first circumnavigation of world
		1491-1556	Ignatius Loyola, Spanish founder of Jesuits		
		1497-1543	Hans Holbein, German painter	1525	Potato introduced to Europe
1505	Portuguese establish trading posts in East Africa	1500-33	Atahualpa, last Inca ruler		
		1505-72	John Knox, Scottish Protestant reformer	1535	Cartier navigates St. Lawrence River
		1512-94	Mercator, Flemish cartographer	1543	Copernicus declares that Earth revolves around Sun around Sun

EUROPE	
1536	Suppression of monasteries begins in England
1545	Council of Trent marks start of Counter-Reformation
1558	England loses Calais to French
1562-98	Wars of Religion in France
1571	Battle of Lepanto: end of Turkish sea power in central Mediterranean
1572	Dutch revolt against Spain,
1588	Spanish Armada defeated by English
1600	English East India Company founded
1605	Gunpowder Plot
1609	Dutch win freedom from Spain
1618-48	Thirty Years' War
1642-6	English Civil War
1648-9	Revolt of Fronde in Paris
1649	Execution of Charles I in London
1667	Beginning of French expansion under Louis XIV
1688	England's 'Glorious Revolution'
1701	Act of Settlement in Britain
1701-13	War of Spanish Succession
1704	Battle of Blenheim
1707	Union of England and Scotland
1713	Treaty of Utrecht
1740-48	War of Austrian Succession
1746	Jacobites defeated at Culloden in Scotland
1756	Start of Seven Year's War
1789	French Revolution
1799	Napoleon becomes French 1st Consul
1804	Napoleon proclaimed Emperor
1805	Battles of Trafalgar and Austerlitz
1812	Napoleon's Russian campaign
1815	Napoleon defeated at Waterloo
1821-29	Greek War of Independence
1830	Revolutions in France, Germany, Poland, Italy. Creation of Belgium
1846	Irish potato famine
1846	Britain repeals Corn Laws
1848	Year of Revolutions

AMERICAS	
1536	Cortes reaches southern California
1541	DeSoto reaches Mississippi River
1565	St. Augustine, Florida colonized by Spanish
1579	Sir Francis Drake lands at San Francisco
1584	Roanoke Island, Virginia is colonized
1591	Roanoke colony mysteriously abandoned
1601	Newfoundland explored by Gosnold
1607	First successful colony in America (Jamestown, Virginia)
1608	French colonists found Quebec
1620	Puritans land in New England
1626	Dutch settle in New Amsterdam
1654	Portuguese take Brazil from Dutch
1664	New Amsterdam seized by British and renamed New York
1693	Gold discovered in Brazil
1759	British capture Quebec from French
1765	Stamp Act in American colonies
1773	Boston Tea Party
1775-78	American War of Independence
1776	Declaration of Independence
1789	George Washington becomes first U.S. president
1791	Slave revolt in Haiti
1803	Louisiana Purchase doubles size of U.S.
1808-28	Independence movements in South America
1819	Spain cedes Florida to U.S.
1836	Texas wins independence from Mexico
1840	Union of Upper and Lower Canada
1848	California Gold Rush begins

ASIA	
1556	Ivan the Terrible conquers Volga basin
1565	Mughal power extended
1644	Ch'ing dynasty founded in China by Manchus
1690	Foundation of Calcutta by British
1707	Break up of Mughal Empire
1724	Hyderabad in India gains freedom from Mughals
1757	Battle of Plassey establishes British rule in India
1775	Peasant uprising in Russia
1783	India Act gives Britain control of India
1799	Napoleon invades Syria
1804-15	Serbs revolt against Turkey
1819	British found Singapore
1830-54	Russia conquers Kazackhstan
1842	Hong Kong ceded to Britain
1845-8	Anglo-Sikh wars in India

AFRICA		PEOPLE		INVENTIONS DISCOVERIES	
1546	Destruction of Mali Empire by Songhai	1443-96	Francis Drake, English sailor		
		1547-1616	Cervantes, Spanish writer	1559	Tobacco introduced to Europe
1570	Bornu Empire in the Sudan flourishes	1548-1614	El Greco, Spanish painter		
1571	Portuguese establish colony in Angola (Southern Africa)				
		1564-1616	William Shakespeare		
		1564-1642	Galileo, Italian astronomer	1577-80	Drake sails round world
				1582	Introduction of Gregorian calendar
		1577-1640	Rubens, Flemish painter	1609	Invention of telescope
1591	Moroccans destroy Songhai Empire	1588-1679	Thomas Hobbes, English philosopher	1618	Imbert (French) reaches Timbuktu
		1596-1650	Descartes, French thinker	1643	Invention of barometer
		1602-61	Mazarin, French statesman		
		1606-69	Rembrandt, Dutch painter		
		1608-74	John Milton, English poet		
		1622-73	Molière, French dramatist		
		1642-1727	Isaac Newton, scientist		
		1643-1715	Reign of Louis XIV		
1652	Foundation of Cape Colony by Dutch	1650-1722	Duke of Marlborough		
		1689-1725	Reign of Peter the Great	1698	Thomas Savery invents steam pump
1686	French annex Madagascar	1685-1750	J.S. Bach, composer		
1705	Turks overthrown in Tunis	1685-1759	Handel, German composer	1709	Darby pioneers iron smelting
		1694-1778	Voltaire, French writer		
		1703-91	John Wesley, English preacher		
		1706-90	Benjamin Franklin, American inventor		
		1712-78	J.J. Rousseau, French philosopher	1712	Thomas Newcomen's steam engine
		1725-74	Robert Clive, ruler in India	1728	Bering discovers Bering Strait
1787	British acquire Sierra Leone	1728-79	James Cook, explorer	1733	John Kay's flying shuttle
		1743-1826	Thomas Jefferson, American statesman	1752	Franklin's lightning conductor
		1756-91	W.A. Mozart, German composer	1764	Hargreave's spinning jenny
		1769-1821	Napoleon Bonaparte	1765	James Watt's steam engine
		1769-1850	Duke of Wellington	1768	Cook begins Pacific exploration
1798	Napoleon attacks Egypt	1770-1827	Beethoven, German composer		
1802-11	Portuguese cross Africa	1776-1830	John Constable, English painter	1782	Watts' double acting steam engine
1807	British abolish slave trade	1783-1830	Simon Bolivar, 'Liberator'	1785	Cartwright's power loom
1811	Mohammad Ali takes control in Egypt	1788-1850	Robert Peel, English statesman	1793	Eli Whitney's cotton gin
1818	Zulu Empire founded in S. Africa	1806-59	I.K. Brunel, British engineer	1805	Mungo Park explores Niger River
1822	Liberia founded for free slaves	1810-61	Cavour, Italian unifier	1815	Davy's miners' safety lamp
1830	French begin conquest of Algeria	1813-83	Richard Wagner, German composer	1825	First passenger steam railway
1835-37	Great Trek of Boers in S. Africa	1815-98	Otto von Bismarck, German statesman	1828	Neilson's blast furnace
				1831	Faraday's dynamo
		1821-90	Richard Burton, explorer	1844	Invention of safety match

EUROPE		AMERICAS		ASIA	
1851	Great Exhibition in London			1850/56	Australia and New Zealand granted responsible governments
1854-6	Crimean War	1861–5	American Civil War	1854	Trade treaty between Japan and US
1860	Unification of Italy begins	1865	U.S. President Abraham Lincoln assassinated	1857	Indian Mutiny
1867	North German Confederation	1867	Dominion of Canada formed	1877	Victoria becomes Empress of India
1870-71	Franco-Prussian War	1876	Battle of Little Big Horn	1885	Indian National Congress formed
1871	Proclamation of German Empire			1886	British annex Burma
1878	Congress of Berlin	1898	Spanish-American War	1894-5	Sino-Japanese war
1822-1914	Triple Alliance between Germany, Austria, Italy	1903	Panama Canal Zone to U.S.	1901	Unification of Australia
				1906	Revolution in Persia
1904	Anglo-French Entente			1910	Japan annexes Korea
1905	First revolution in Russia	1911	Mexican Revolution	1911	Chinese revolution under Sun Yat-sen
1912-13	Balkan Wars	1914	Panama Canal opens	1917	Balfour Declaration promises Jewish homeland
1914-18	First World War	1917	U.S. enters World War I		
1917	Russian Revolution			1922	Republic proclaimed in Turkey
1919	Treaty of Versailles			1926	Chiang Kai-shek unites China
1920	League of Nations established			1931	Japanese occupy Manchuria
1922	Irish Free State created			1934	Mao Tse-tung's Long March in China
1926	General Strike in Britain	1929	Wall Street Crash	1937	Japanese capture Peking
1931	Spain becomes a republic	1933	Roosevelt introduces New Deal in U.S.	1940	Japan allies with Germany
1933	Hitler becomes German Chancellor			1945	First A-bombs dropped on Japan
1936-9	Spanish Civil War			1946-9	Civil war in China
1938	Germany occupies Austria			1947	India and Pakistan independent
1939-45	Second World War	1941	U.S. enters World War II	1956	Arab-Israeli war
1945	United Nations established	1950	U.S. enters Korean War	1957	Malaysia independent
		1959	Cuban revolution	1962	Sino-Indian war
1949	Formation of NATO	1962	Cuban missile crisis	1965	United States sends troops to Vietnam
1955	Warsaw Pact signed	1963	President John F. Kennedy assassinated	1971	East Pakistan becomes Bangladesh
1957	European Common Market set up	1965	U.S. sends troops to Vietnam	1973	Arab-Israeli war
1961	Berlin Wall built	1968	Martin Luther King, Jr. assassinated	1974	Portuguese African colonies independent
1963	Nuclear Test Ban Treaty	1969	U.S. astronauts first to land on moon	1979	Shah of Iran deposed
1968	Russian troops in Czechoslovakia	1970	Ceasefire in Vietnam. U.S. troops begin to come home	1980	Iran-Iraq war
1973	Britain, Eire and Denmark join European Economic Community	1972–75	Watergate break-in and investigations		
1975	Monarchy restored in Spain	1974	President Richard Nixon resigns		
1978	John Paul II elected as first non-Italian Pope for over 450 years	1978	U.S. agrees to diplomatic relations with China and ends those with Taiwan		
		1981	U.S. hostages held in Iran and released after 444 days		

AFRICA		
1860	French expansion in West Africa	
1869	Opening of Suez Canal	
1875	Disraeli buys Suez Canal shares	
1879	Zulu War	
1882	British occupy Egypt	
1884	Germany acquires African colonies	
1885	Belgium acquires Congo	
1886	Germany and Britain divide E. Africa	
1899-1902	Anglo-Boer War	
1909	Union of South Africa formed	
1911	Italians conquer Libya	
1914	British Protectorate in Egypt	
1919	Nationalist revolt in Egypt	
1922	Egypt becomes independent	
1936	Italy annexes Ethiopia	
1949	Apartheid established in South Africa	
1956	Suez crisis	
1957	Ghana becomes independent, followed by other African States	
1967-70	Nigerian civil war	
1979	General Amin flees from Uganda	
1980	Last British colony in Africa achieves independence as Zimbabwe	

PEOPLE	
1828-1910	Leo Tolstoy, Russian writer
1837-1901	Reign of Queen Victoria
1840-1926	Claude Monet, French painter
1840-1917	Rodin, French sculptor
1853-1902	Cecil Rhodes, colonizer
1856-1939	Sigmund Freud, psychoanalyst
1858-1928	Emmeline Pankhurst, women's leader
1860-1904	Anton Checkhov, Russian playwright
1863-1947	Henry Ford, US car maker
1866-1925	Sun Yat-sen, Chinese statesman
1872-1928	Roald Amundsen, explorer
1874-1965	Winston Churchill, British statesman
1881-1973	Pablo Picasso, Spanish painter
1883-1945	Mussolini, Italian dictator
1889-1945	Adolf Hitler, German Nazi leader
1889-1964	Nehru, Indian leader
1892-1975	Franco, Spanish dictator
1893-1976	Mao Tse-tung, Chinese revolutionary
1913–	Willy Brandt, German statesman
1914-	Thor Heyerdahl, explorer
1921-	John Glenn, first American in space
1922-	Julius Nyerere, Tanzanian leader
1924-	Kenneth Kaunda, Zambian leader
1926-	Fidel Castro, Cuban leader
1930-	Neil Armstrong, first on moon
1934-68	Yuri Gagarin, first in space

INVENTIONS DISCOVERIES	
1853-6	Livingstone crosses Africa
1855	Bessemer's Converter
1859	Lake Tanganyika discovered
1862	Gatling's rapid fire gun
1866	Nobel invents dynamite
1871	Stanley finds Livingstone
1876	Bell invents telephone
1884	Waterman's fountain pen
1886-7	Benz and Daimler invent internal combustion engine
1895	Marconi's wireless
1903	First successful flight by Wright brothers
1909	Peary reaches North Pole
1911	Amundsen reaches South Pole
1913	Geiger counter invented
1918	Automatic rifle invented
1919	Rutherford splits atom
1919	First crossing of Atlantic by air
1925	Baird invents television
1926	First liquid fuel rocket
1930	Whittle's jet engine
1935	Invention of nylon
1939	Development of penicillin
1947	First supersonic flight
1948	Transistor developed
1953	The conquest of Everest
1957	First satellite launched
1961	First man in space
1969	First man lands on Moon
1976	Microcomputers on a single chip

Index

Acknowledgement is made for the use of the following photographs: 10 Ronald Sheridan; 26 William MacQuitty; Society for Anglo-Chinese Understanding; 37 Michael Holford; 41 Zefa; 42 Sonia Halliday; 46 Universitets Oldsaksamling, Oslo; 48 National Travel Association of Denmark; 62 Marian Morrison; 63 Tony Morrison; 88 Giraudon; 89 Mansell Collection; 113 Birmingham Museums and Art Gallery.